# Racing the Sun

## Paul Pitts

AN AVON CAMELOT BOOK

AVON BOOKS, INC.
1350 Avenue of the Americas
New York, New York 10019

Copyright © 1988 by Paul Pitts
Published by arrangement with the author
Visit our website at http://www.AvonBooks.com
Library of Congress Catalog Card Number: 88-91510
ISBN: 0-380-75496-7
RL: 5.2

First Avon Camelot Printing: August 1988

CAMELOT TRADEMARK REG. U.S. PAT. OFF. AND IN OTHER COUNTRIES, MARCA REGISTRADA, HECHO EN U.S.A.

Printed in the U.S.A.

OPM 30 29 28 27 26

For my
mother and father,
who taught me
important things

Although I've lived many years in close contact with the Navajo people (the past thirteen years, right on the reservation), I'm still learning about their culture. I am greatly indebted to the following friends and staff members at Montezuma Creek School who read the manuscript of RACING THE SUN and offered suggestions to ensure its authenticity to Navajo life: Louise A. Burke, Lyndell Chee, Cita Holly, Genevieve Jackson, Ethel Jones, Glenna Sam, and Steward Sam.

I also wish to thank the following friends whose time and assistance were invaluable: DeAnn Forbes, K.C. Benedict, Sandra Skousen, Beth Eck, Sheila Gill, and Lisa Nidey.

I thank my wife, Kathleen, for her encouragement, support, and careful reading.

# Note to the Reader

Navajo is primarily a spoken language. Although there are several bilingual schools on the reservation which include Navajo language as part of their curriculum, the majority of Navajos still do not read or write it. I have included a number of Navajo words and phrases in this book because they would come naturally to the characters. It was necessary to change the spelling of some of these words.

Navajo has a sound called "slashed L." It is made by placing your tongue behind your front teeth and blowing air around the sides of the tongue. The closest English sound is *th*, so rather than make up a new letter, I changed the slashed L sounds to *th*. For example, a word such as *hataałii* will be shown in the book as *hataathlii*.

Navajo frequently has a stopping of breath which is called a "glottal stop." The closest I can come in describing this is the action of catching your breath in surprise. It is a little like a soft hiccup. The glottal stop is shown by a ´ in the Navajo word. I have included glottal stops in my modified spelling.

One other spelling change was made. When a *t* is combined with slashed L and a glottal stop, the resulting sound is like a very harsh *cl,* as in the word "click." The spelling of little goat, *kl´ izi yazhi*, should officially be *tl´ izi yazhi*.

There also may be some confusion over the Navajo use of endearments and terms of respect. *Shiyaazh* is *my son* when a woman talks to her child. *Shiye'* is *my son* when a man is speaking. *Shiyazhi* is a term of endearment that anyone can use. It is like "little one." Older folks use it quite often when talking to children and grandchildren. *Shichei* means *my grandfather* when speaking to your mother's father. It is also used as a title of respect for any older man whether he is related to you or not.

*Paul Pitts*
*Montezuma Creek, Utah*
*1988*

# Chapter One

"I don't know why I keep taking a chance on you," Ham said, shifting his books to the other arm. "It must be pity."

The time had come for his customary lecture.

"It's certainly not your good looks or your money; you don't have either one."

"Come on. If we split the assignment, we each end up doing only half the work," I said.

"Or your enthusiasm for academic challenge."

He stopped and looked at me for a few seconds. "All right, you win. I'll do the even-numbered problems, you do the odd."

I took a quick peek at page 277 in my algebra book. "You do the odd and I'll do the even."

"What difference does it make?"

"I just like even numbers," I said. I knew he'd find out later that there were thirty-five problems. Eventually it would dawn on him that whoever did the odd-numbered

1

ones would end up doing the extra problem, but he wouldn't mind. He's better at math than I am.

"This time I expect you to finish your half of the assignment, Cochise." Ham pushed back the tangle of curly brown hair that always hung in front of his eyes. "And if you don't mind, try to get the answers right for a change."

"I will do my very best."

"I was afraid of that," he said, but I caught his crooked grin.

"If you think about it, Ham, the work we're doing isn't that important. There's only three weeks of school left and Thompson isn't even recording our scores anymore." I offered him a stick of gum, but he shook his head. "I think he has our grades already filled out. Everybody's into their end-of-the-school-year coast."

I threw my gum wrapper on the sidewalk.

"It's a matter of honor," Ham said, stopping to pick it up.

Littering that way was just a test. I wanted to see if he was still into heavy-duty ecological protection. I was going to pick it up if he didn't. Maybe.

"Honor? If you're not careful, Berger, you'll be thrown out of the Underachievers." I reached up with my free hand and lowered it three times, like a train engineer pulling the whistle cord. "Uga, uga, uga," I chanted, then produced a resonant snoring sound.

That was the official sign of UGA, the Underachieving Goof-offs of America. I'd organized the club at the beginning of the school year while I was telling Ham about my parents' conversation from the previous night. My mother had just returned from a parent-teacher conference, and I happened to be standing outside their bedroom door.

"Almost every teacher says that Brandon is an underachiever," Mom reported.

"Underachieving is just a fancy way of saying lazy," my dad said in his usual supportive manner.

Ham's the only other member of UGA. It's a very exclusive organization. He repeated the chant, and we both ended up laughing. Ham and I have been best friends for four years, since third grade when Mrs. Hunsaker chose us to take down the Thanksgiving display in the hall. I'd never met anyone who could stretch so much time out of so little work. Through Ham's ingenuity, we spent an hour taking down twenty-seven paper-bag turkeys. We missed cursive writing and a Christmas-wreath puzzle page that practiced subtraction. It was great.

I appreciate the fact that Ham likes me the way I am. I can do all sorts of goofy things without being embarrassed. I also get by with calling him Ham, even though his name is David. Of course, his mother wouldn't be so crazy about her only son going through Roosevelt Jr. High School with the nickname of Ham Berger, so I have to be careful when I'm around his parents.

The acceptance is reciprocal. I let him pass on some pretty bizarre behavior, too. And if my mother knew he called me Cochise, along with ninety percent of the student body at Roosevelt, she'd have a heart attack. I'm Indian, actually Navajo. I know Cochise was an Apache, but Ham didn't know any famous Navajos. As a matter of fact, I don't know any either. Maybe my dad—he's not really famous, but he's successful. He teaches at the University of Utah.

3

I'm Navajo like Ham is Jewish. He calls himself "a cultural observer" as opposed to a participant. His family observes some of the Jewish holidays, when it's convenient, but they aren't regular about that stuff. They went to Ham's cousin Theo's bar mitzvah last fall, but when his other cousin had his day in the spotlight, Mr. Berger was out of town and Mrs. Berger's old roommate from college was visiting, so they didn't go.

I guess if I'm honest about it, I'm not even an observer of Navajo culture. Even though both my dad and mom are Navajo, they've set their sights on the American dream—two cars in the driveway, a TV in each bedroom, and a pool in the backyard. That's quite different from the Navajo dream—an old pickup truck, three sheepskins in every hogan, and a herd of goats in the backyard. So far, we have the two cars, a TV in the family room, but no swimming pool.

When we turned the corner, I saw my dad's car already parked in the driveway. He was early for a change. We crossed the lawn and were heading around to the side door, the shortest route to the kitchen and cookies and milk, when we heard my parents' loud voices. Actually we didn't hear both of my parents. My dad would yell something, then there would be a pause while my mother replied, then my dad would yell again.

"I think I'll skip the snack," Ham said.

"Are you going to let a little family discussion chase you away from my mom's chocolate-chip cookies?"

There was another rumble from inside, punctuated with guttural clatter, then silence.

"What was he saying, anyway?" Ham asked.

"Search me; it's Navajo."

Ham looked skyward. "I know it's Navajo, you dope.

**4**

If they were talking English, I'd know what the fight was about."

I heard my dad's voice again, a little softer but still angry.

"Some Indian you are, Cochise!"

I was going to mention that if they were fighting in Hebrew and he was interpreting, we still wouldn't know what the fight was about, but my mom's voice interrupted. It was the first time we'd been able to hear her, and even though we couldn't understand what she said, we could tell she was mad. Then a door slammed, and the house was silent again. In a few seconds another door closed.

"I have cookies and milk at my house," Ham offered. "Want to come over for a little while?"

"And miss out on this tidbit of family intrigue?" I grinned, and Ham laughed.

"See you around." He turned and headed down the driveway. "Don't forget to do the even-numbered problems."

"I'll call you later."

He reached the street. "I'll do the extra problem . . . as usual," he called. As he disappeared behind the neighbor's hedge I heard, "Uga, Uga, Uga."

I listened at the door for a minute for new rumblings from my parents' fight, but I knew there wouldn't be any. They didn't fight very often, but when they did, doors slamming in separate rooms always signaled the end of open battle and the beginning of a silent cold war. My mom was so mellow that she put up with a lot from my dad. The issue had to be important for her to get involved. Good grief! She had even raised her voice!

Standing on the porch guessing at the problem wasn't

giving me any answers. I went in the kitchen, making sure the door slammed so they'd know I was home. Usually my mom comes out and asks me how my day was. What she really wants to know is whether or not I got into any trouble. Then she asks about homework. Both she and Dad have this crazy idea that my whole future, maybe the future of the entire free world, rests on my getting straight A's on my report card.

When she didn't come out of her room, I yelled, "I'm home!" No response, so I headed for my own room. As I went through the dining room, I noticed an envelope on the table. The return address was Little Water. That's where my dad was born. It's on the Navajo reservation, and my dad would just as soon forget there was such a place. I had this feeling that the letter was the cause of the argument. My dad goes berserk whenever he's reminded of his Navajo background.

When he was growing up on the reservation, my father's name was Kee Redhouse. He left home to go to high school at a government boarding school and discovered the enticingly affluent world of White society. He started calling himself Keith. By the time he was accepted into graduate school, the Redhouse had evolved into Rogers. I guess he thought that Dr. Rogers sounded more American than Dr. Redhouse. He isn't an open-your-mouth-and-say-aahh kind of doctor. He's a Ph.D., a university professor. He also writes books and magazine articles. That's why I said he was kind of famous. I've never read more than a paragraph of stuff he's written because it's all pretty boring. Dad's an engineer. I was little when I found out he was an engineer, and I got all excited. Then I found out he didn't have anything to do with trains, and the glamour disappeared.

I might have had a little more contact with Navajo life through my mother, but she doesn't have any family left. She was raised on the reservation by her great aunt, who died when Mom was in high school, and she hasn't been back to her home there since. I asked Mom if she knew Dad when he was Kee Redhouse. She just smiled and said, "The Navajo reservation is a pretty big place." It's almost as big as West Virginia and straddles the border between Arizona and New Mexico. Mom was raised in the western part, and my dad's home is in New Mexico.

I went to my room, slipped a Van Halen tape into the stereo, and turned the volume up. That never fails to bring my folks running. They aren't rock fans, just "trying to keep the plaster on the walls." That's my dad's phrase. I didn't want their attention because I was lonely, but I hate to be left out of a family crisis. Usually, the higher the volume, the faster their response time, but after five minutes neither one had shown up to yell at me, so I turned it down.

Sitting at my desk, I flipped open my algebra book and copied down equation number two. I got the answer from the back of the book and wrote it down a few lines below the problem. Then I tried to work my way back from the answer to the problem. Whoever invented algebra had a very twisted mind. He was probably locked in a prison cell, solitary confinement, no doubt. He not only had nothing better to do, but he wanted to get back at the world. I finally had to give in and look at the examples that came before the problems and try to remember what Ham had explained to me in class. The honorable David Berger has a twisted mind and relates well to algebraic equations, did I mention that?

After I figured out the pattern, it really wasn't so hard. I got to number thirty-four in no time.

I turned up the stereo again with no results, so I turned it down and picked up my phone to call Ham. His line was busy. Just as well, because he'd probably want to know what caused the fireworks at my house. It was time to do a little detective work. On my way to the kitchen, I picked up the letter from Little Water. As usual, the envelope was addressed to my dad "and family," so I figured it was OK to read what was inside. The letter was from my Aunt Ethel, my dad's older sister. She's the one who keeps in touch with us most often. She writes to my dad "and family," and my mom answers her letters.

Aunt Ethel didn't waste any time on the weather; she jumped right to the business at hand. "Your father is very sick," I read. "We have tried to get him to go to the doctors in town, but he won't go. He is getting weaker all the time. He won't stay with us. He needs to have someone around to take care of him. If I bring him over to my home, he will just try to go back to his place every day. Besides, I have to work and there isn't anyone to watch out for him around here. Helen is home all day and your father would be close to a doctor and the care he needs."

She went on about how she could help out with expenses and how she was only asking now because it was an emergency. She hoped to hear from my dad as soon as he made up his mind.

I got a glass of milk and a handful of cookies and went back to my room. No wonder my father was acting a little crazy! Having my grandfather come to live with us could cause a major household upheaval. We couldn't

**8**

even have a dog, because Dad said it would upset the balance of our family life.

Ham will love this drama-in-real-life, I thought, picking up the phone. His mother answered on the first ring.

"Is David there?"

"Just a minute, I'll get him." I heard her yelling his name. "How are you, Brandon?" Mrs. Berger is very friendly; she always asks me how I'm doing.

"Not so great, Mrs. Berger."

"That's nice." She always asks, but she never listens to the answer. I test her every once in a while.

"Here's David now."

"What's up?"

"They want my grandpa to come live with us."

"Who does? Your mom and dad?"

"Of course not. The rest of the family, my dad's brothers and sister who live on the reservation." I bit into a cookie. "He's not doing so great healthwise, and there's nobody to take care of him down there, so they want him to come live here for a while."

"Do you think your folks will say it's OK?"

"That's probably what the fight's about."

"Your dad wants his father to come and your mom hates the idea?"

"I'll bet it's the other way around. My mom's probably the one who thinks we ought to take him in. She's very big on family stuff."

"So who's going to win?"

"My dad. He'll either sulk until my mom gives in to him or he'll be a terrible grouch until she sees that Grandpa would be miserable if he came to stay."

"He must take lessons from my mother." I could hear the smile in Ham's voice. "What do you think?

9

Would you like to have your grandfather living with you guys?"

"I'm not sure, I don't even know him. We only go down there once a year, usually on our way to someplace else. After a couple of hours my dad gets the urge to leave."

"Does he fight with your grandfather?"

"I don't think so. My dad just acts uncomfortable. Grandpa talks to him in Navajo and Dad answers in English. I don't know what Grandpa says but my dad's end of the conversation is always pretty boring."

"If he lived in your house, you'd get to know your grandfather better."

"Maybe I would but maybe not. We don't have all that much to talk about. One thing's for sure, it'll be crowded around here. In case you haven't noticed, this isn't exactly Buckingham Palace."

"So, make a list."

"A list?"

"I always make a list when I can't decide something. Write down the good things about your grandfather coming to live here and then write down the bad things. It'll help you make up your mind."

Trust Ham. He's a methodical marvel.

"I don't know, Ham. I usually take a more spontaneous, intuitive approach to life."

He laughed. "You mean you're just too lazy to make a list."

I laughed myself. It's hard to fool a fellow member of UGA. Pans clattered in the kitchen.

"I'd better go find out the details of this crisis. When I learn more, I'll call you back. In the meantime, I'll try your list idea."

**10**

"Right."

I started lowering the receiver. "Hey!" I heard Ham call.

"What?"

"Did you finish your algebra problems?"

"Of course. I finished them and they're all 100 percent correct."

"Well, this day is just full of surprises!"

I hung up and took my milk glass into the kitchen.

"So, how was your day?" I asked my mother. She gave me her say-one-more-word-and-you're-dead look, so I went back to my room, pulled out a notebook, and started my list.

# Chapter Two

Once in a while, we have a focus-on-Brandon meal. Every question, every phrase of conversation is directed to me. My parents won't talk to each other, but they need to fill the empty room with sound. I guess it's better than complete silence, but it doesn't make for maximum digestive efficiency for any of us. I'm glad it doesn't happen very often.

"Brandon, will you pass the vegetables," my dad said. I reached over, picked up the bowl of green beans that was in front of my mother's plate, and passed it to him.

"How was school today?" Mom asked.

"Fine." I speared a couple of beans. "I've finished my homework," I said, spoiling the next topic of conversation.

"Good," Dad said.

It was quiet for a few minutes. My folks know all that psychological stuff about how damaging it is to bottle

13

up your emotions, but they forget it when they have a relationship crisis. I took it upon myself to help them release some of that tension.

"I notice we got a letter from Little Water," I began. "How's everything down on the old homestead, Dad?"

They looked at one another.

"Fine," Dad said. "Everything's fine. Eat your dinner."

I already had my mouth full of casserole and a forkful of beans on the way.

My mom said, "Your grandfather might be coming to stay."

Dad looked over at her quickly.

"Just for a little while," she added.

"Grandpa?" I sounded convincingly surprised. "Staying with us? How come?" There are times when I think I should channel my creative energy toward a career on the stage.

"He's not feeling very well."

"They've got perfectly good nursing homes down there, Helen." My father put down his fork. "Dad would be closer to his home, closer to his family . . ." It sounded like he'd been making his own list.

"We're his family, too, Keith."

They forgot all about me. I knew they would. I get this great feeling of power each time I manipulate my environment and produce the exact results I anticipated. It's like being the mastermind behind the Super Bowl. No matter who wins, it's always an exciting game. I settled back to watch the action.

"Can you imagine your father in a nursing home?"

"Can you picture him here? He'd disrupt our whole life." Dad's kickoff.

14

Mom laid her fork down. "Things would change a little, of course, but . . ."

"Who's going to take care of him?"

"I don't mind making sure he's comfortable, that he eats . . ."

"How about taking him to the bathroom, do you mind that, Helen? Do you mind cleaning up after him if he gets an upset stomach after lunch or soils himself because you're busy with your roses, or friends, or clubs, and forget to take him to the bathroom?"

"Don't invent problems until we find out how sick he really is, Keith."

My dad was really charging toward the end zone. "What about our friends? Are you ready for the funny looks we'll get because our house smells like a hogan? What about entertaining? Let's get a good story ready to explain the singing, the chanting from the other room that interrupts dinner conversation."

"He won't chant, honey." Mom laughed, but it didn't slow down my father.

"He chants, Helen. He not only knows all that traditional mumbo jumbo, he believes it. He practices it . . . daily."

My mother shrugged. "What if he does? What happened to all your enlightened broad-mindedness? I'll do my thing and the rest of the world can do their thing? If your father wants to practice his religion with stories and chants, we can give him that right."

"That's my point. He can do his thing, but if he does it here, in my house, he infringes on my rights—on our rights—to live the way we want without being embarrassed."

My parents picked up their water glasses at the same time and took sips.

My dad hadn't even set his glass down before he said, "Where's he going to stay, Helen? Do you want to build a new room onto the house? Shall we give up the patio? Your rose bed?"

Dad was really scrambling for yardage with that one, because my mother loves her roses. When it comes down to buying special fertilizer for the roses or an extra bag of cookies for me, the roses always win.

"I think you're anticipating problems that may never exist." Mom's voice was getting calmer and softer, the way it does when she's very serious—and very sure of getting her way. "Maybe he won't be happy here, maybe he'll insist on going back, even if it's to a nursing home. On the other hand, we might have to add on an extra room, even a whole apartment. Let's take this problem one step at a time. Couldn't you just give up the den for a few months while we see if he's going to stay, how the whole situation is going to work out?"

My dad just sat there and pushed beans around his plate.

"He's your father, Keith," Mom said, stopping him cold on the one-yard line.

"All right, I could give up the den. Of course I could do that." He took another sip of water. "But it will take time to move everything out and fix it up to provide any kind of comfort. I think Ethel expects some action right away." He picked up his glass, didn't drink, and put it down again. "*If* we decide that it's best for Dad to come and live with us."

I grabbed my napkin and wiped my mouth so he'd

**16**

miss the grin. He doesn't like to give up a fight too easily.

"In the meantime, he can stay with Brandon, in his room." My mother started her play.

"Now, wait a minute—" I began. I didn't mind if Grandpa came to visit, but I hadn't known sharing my room would be part of the deal. "I don't think Grandpa wants to be scrunched in that little room with all my stuff, my friends always crowding in there, my stereo cracking the plaster. He's probably used to wide-open spaces and the peace and quiet of isolation."

It was Mom's turn to smile. "Everybody will have to give a little and adjust. We'll just grow to make the best of a challenging situation." Trust my mother to look at mammoth inconvenience as a chance to develop character. I don't care if she develops her own character and gives up her rose garden, but I like my own character to be small and compact, kind of modern, not old-fashioned and bulky, and I hadn't anticipated my character being developed at this early age.

"After dinner we'll let the dishes sit and get the other bunk bed from the garage. Then we can start cleaning and arranging Brandon's room."

"There's no need to rush into this thing and start moving furniture," Dad said.

"There's no need to put it off, either." Mom knew she'd better get moving while she had the advantage.

My father and I looked at each other. We knew the game was as good as over.

"You two get the bed; I'll call the trading post and leave a message for Ethel," Dad said. "She's probably been checking there every day since she mailed that letter."

**17**

The trading post isn't like you see in movies. It's just a store. It's also the Little Water social center. People get their mail there, and almost everybody stops by to visit and keep up with the local news. Aunt Ethel would get the message there and could call my dad within a day or two.

"If you've had enough to eat, let's get busy," Mom said to me.

I thought about putting it off by stuffing another helping of casserole down my throat, but that would only prolong the agony. "Can I call David first? It's about our homework."

"I thought you had your homework finished."

"I do, but maybe I forgot something."

"Call him after we get things done."

"I want to tell him about Grandpa coming."

"The whole world doesn't need to know about this," my dad said. "Let's wait and take things one step at a time, like your mother suggested. Maybe your grandfather won't even want to come up here."

"Then maybe we should wait to move the bed."

"To the garage, Brandon," Mom said.

I left my father looking solemnly at the casserole hardening on his plate and followed her.

By the time we brought the bed frame, springs, and mattress from the garage to my room, Dad had already called the Little Water trading post and was deep into some article in one of his engineering journals. Mom didn't want to bother him, so we bolted the bunk bed together by ourselves and set things up. My mother is a very independent woman. Because she's so independent and can do lots of things on her own, my dad has a pretty soft life. He doesn't have to do the stuff that most

**18**

fathers have to do—yard work, fixing the TV antenna, putting lights on a Christmas tree.

I have this theory about family organization. There are two roles for parents: the Doer and the Done For. In my family, Dad is the Done For. In the Berger family, Mrs. Berger is the Done For. When we Rogerses go out for a hamburger, it's my mom who goes into McDonald's to get the food. When I go with Ham's family, I notice it's his dad who does that job. Mrs. Berger stays in the car like my father. I asked Dad about it once. He said he wasn't lazy, it was just that families develop their own patterns of responsibilities. I'm going to make sure I line myself up with the Done For's responsibilities when I have my own family.

The bunk bed from the garage looked a lot newer than my bed, so we put it on the top because it shows more than the bottom bunk. When they bought the bunk beds, I think my folks thought they might have another little Rogers to share it with me. Nobody anticipated that my roommate would be a seventy-eight-year-old Redhouse. Mom insisted on having matching bedspreads.

"Flowers?" I said.

"That's all we have, Brandon."

"But, Mom, flowers are so . . ." I tried to find the right word.

"I'll see if I can find something different on sale," she promised. "This is just temporary."

"At least Grandpa will have his privacy." I sighed. "If you think I'm bringing my friends in here to sit on this sissy bed . . ."

She smiled. "Now, let's see what we can eliminate from your drawers and closets to make room for Grandpa's things."

"How about letting me do that myself?"

"Are you stalling?"

"No, really, Mom. I'll clean out the drawers tonight and box up what I don't need. And I'll do the closet tomorrow."

"I don't mind helping, Brandon."

"That's OK. It's my junk." I opened my miscellaneous drawer and quickly closed it again, but not before my mother got a good look and winced. "I know you're anxious to get to the dishes."

She smiled. "You're so thoughtful."

Mom looked around at my posters. "Don't forget to take these rock stars down."

"Now, wait a minute! This is still my room. I ought to have some say about how it's decorated."

"Just take them down for now and when we get Grandpa's room fixed up, you can put them back."

"I really don't want to take them down!" I tried to keep my voice even, but the volume rose all on its own.

"I'm not asking you to make a major change here, Brandon."

"Those posters are important to me, Mom."

My dad came in.

"What's the problem?"

"I just want Brandon to take down his posters for a little while, until your father gets settled in."

I waited for Dad to make his your-mother-has-a-good-point speech.

"I think he ought to have the right to keep his posters up," Dad said.

Mom just looked at him.

"You do?" I asked.

"Of course I do. This is your room, Brandon."

"I just think we ought to make sure that your dad feels welcome," Mom said. "If we all just give a little . . ."

"You keep talking about everybody giving a little, Helen. Well, Dad is going to have to give a little, too. We'll do everything we can to make him know that we're glad to have him live with us, but I'm not about to change our whole life-style to please him. I've worked too hard for it. If he doesn't like some things around here . . ."

We waited for him to finish.

". . . he can just . . . give a little."

"Well, we've got time to think about the posters. Maybe I'm rushing things," Mom said. "Let's wait a day or so and decide." She picked up the pliers and moved toward the door.

Dad went back to the den, and Mom turned to me. "Don't put off getting ready for Grandpa, Brandon . . . your drawers and closet. I know you're not exactly thrilled about having a roommate, but I only have enough energy to push your father on this thing. I need your cooperation."

"How come Dad doesn't like Grandpa?"

She came over and pulled me to the bed to sit next to her. "Your father likes Grandpa, Brandon. He loves your grandfather. It's just that . . ."

She put her arm around me.

"It's very complicated, but let me try to explain. When your dad left the reservation to go to school, he decided that the White way of living was the way to become successful. He threw himself totally into attaining that success. In fact, he hardly went home at all. When he did visit, he found himself dissatisfied with everything at home and restless to get back to what he calls civilization."

She started scratching my back like she used to when I was a little kid. It still felt good.

"I think your father has been fighting so hard to break away from the reservation and what he feels are the disadvantages of being Navajo that now, even after he's gained the success he was looking for, he can't give up the fight. He can't see anything good about traditional ways.

"And your grandfather is just the opposite. He feels like the White man's way has lured his son away from all that is good, the Navajo way of life."

I pulled my shirttail out so Mom could reach under my shirt and give my back a good scratch. "It's kind of a war."

"Right," Mom said. "Maybe having your grandfather live here will give them a chance to negotiate a peace treaty."

"Or kill each other," I said.

Mom gave me a halfhearted smile, but neither one of us laughed.

# Chapter Three

"I'll tell you all about it when we get home," I told Ham on the phone the next Saturday morning. We were going down to the bus station to meet my grandfather. Most people have this false notion that Indians are slow moving unless they're attacking a wagon train. That's not true, look at my Aunt Ethel. She had Grandpa's bus ticket already in hand when she returned my dad's call. She probably had his bags packed, too.

"You'll have to come over later and meet my grandfather," I said.

"Does he speak English?"

"Of course he does, dope. This isn't a Hollywood Western."

"Just asking. I was afraid I'd have to depend on you to translate." Ham laughed.

"Very funny."

My mother came in.

"I've got to go. We're ready to leave. Come over later."

"I'll be there."

I hung up and watched Mom check herself in the mirror on my closet door. She was wearing a burgundy dress and a silver necklace, bracelet, and earrings, all with turquoise stones—her "Indian jewelry," my dad calls them.

"Wow!" I said, and she smiled. "You look like you're going somewhere a little fancier than the bus station."

"Thank you. I guess that's a compliment." She looked at me for a few seconds. "You look like you're going to a rock concert. How about changing?"

I was wearing jeans and my Twisted Sister T-shirt.

"Oh, Mom."

"Come on, Brandon. You don't want to shock your grandfather the minute he steps off the bus." She glanced at the posters on the walls. "Let's wait till he gets home."

I'd won the Battle of the Rock Posters. Actually, it was a draw. I maintained the right to keep up three pictures, but I had to let her hang a travel poster of Monument Valley. "For balance," she explained.

"I would really appreciate your cooperation just one more time," Mom said. "I practically had to carry your father to the car, and he's sitting there now racing the engine in protest. Just hurry and change your shirt before he comes back in to see what's holding us up. I may not be able to get him out there again."

"You know, Mom, giving in to you is getting to be a habit," I said, pulling on a plain black sweatshirt over Twisted Sister.

"Don't get my hopes up." She was grinning.

We went out the door just as Dad was climbing out of the car.

"Let's go," Mom said, hurrying around to her side of the car.

Dad looked longingly toward the house.

The ride to the bus station was quiet. Any thoughts about Grandpa's visit had already been expressed.

"If we can't find a parking place in front of the station, I'll just drive around the block until you come out," my father said.

I thought my mother would start in again about "making Grandpa feel welcome" and "sharing the responsibility." I'd heard those phrases about four million times in the last few days. But she just sat there and looked out the window.

There were plenty of empty spaces. "I guess I'm in luck," Dad said. My mother smiled.

Dad took his time putting coins into the parking meter and then stayed behind us as we went into the station. Mom and I slowed down so he could catch up, but he didn't. When my mother went over to the counter to ask if Grandpa's bus would be on time, Dad hung around the magazine rack, reading covers. He was certainly being antisocial.

I walked over to browse with him. I was glad I'd hidden Twisted Sister, or he might have moved away from me.

"Any minute now," Mom reported as she joined us. "Let's go over to the door."

"I'll be there in a little while," Dad said.

Mom looked at him. "Come on, Brandon," she said. "Let's meet your grandfather."

"Dad doesn't seem too excited about meeting Grandpa," I said as we stood around watching for the bus.

"I think he's just scared."

"Scared of Grandpa?"

"Maybe scared isn't the right word. I think he's worried about the responsibility of taking care of his father, getting along with him."

"I think Dad's mad because having Grandpa live with us is going to mess up things."

"How about you? Are you mad?"

"I'm just cautious," I said. "I like your idea of taking one day at a time and not looking for trouble. Besides, I'm just a kid. It's you and Dad that have to do most of the work about making sure Grandpa likes it here."

Mom smiled.

I went on. "I just hope Grandpa doesn't start telling Dad all the things he's doing wrong, like back on the reservation."

"You've got to realize that your grandfather is just reminding us about things that are very important to him." Mom stepped forward and checked for the bus. "Maybe the reason your father gets so upset is that some of what Grandpa says makes sense to him."

I hadn't thought of that.

"I think your dad wants your grandfather to approve of how he's living, the decisions he's made."

"What's wrong with the way we live?"

Mom opened her purse, found some mints, and offered me one. "Nothing's wrong with it, it's just so different from the way your father was raised, the way Grandpa and the rest of the family live."

26

"If Grandpa doesn't like it, he knows what he can do about it."

Mom just looked at me.

Finally I said, "Those guys at Little Water aren't exactly living in hogans and riding mustangs bareback, you know. They have pickups and VCRs and pretty nice homes."

"That's true. With their satellite dish, Ethel and Stan get more channels on their TV than we do with cable. I have a feeling that the biggest difference in the way we live and the way your grandfather would like us to live isn't physical, even though we have things a little easier than the others financially."

"Then what are you talking about?"

"I guess our life is different because we're isolated."

She saw I didn't know what she was talking about, and I could tell she was in the process of thinking things through herself.

"The Navajo way of life is based on family, Brandon. Not just a mother and a father and children, but the whole extended family—grandparents, great-grandparents, aunts, uncles, cousins, on and on and on. Everything is shared—money, food, worries, good times."

"Dad shares with those guys. He's always sending money down to Little Water. Remember last Christmas? It cost thirty dollars just to pay the postage on the packages that went down that way."

My mother looked for her roll of mints again, even though she had one in her mouth. Finally she said, almost to herself, "He shares *things* with them, but he doesn't share himself."

I wanted to talk more about it, find out exactly what

**27**

she meant. I think I was starting to understand, but Grandpa's bus roared into the parking port.

We saw my grandfather before he saw us. He was sitting by the window, looking straight ahead. Even after everyone else had left the bus, he sat there.

Dad joined us with a hopeful "No Tom Redhouse?"

I pointed to the bus window.

Grandpa turned his head just then and noticed us. He didn't smile or wave or anything; he just stood up slowly and moved toward the front of the bus. The driver was still standing at the door. Reaching up, he took Grandpa's hand and helped him down the stairs. The old man stood there for a minute, and we stayed where we were, too, watching him.

He looked the same as the last time I'd seen him— gray-and-white hair worn in a traditional bun at the back of his head, unlined bronze face, earrings made of tiny bone beads with a single turquoise stone, the same straight posture—but somehow he had gotten old. The blue plaid flannel shirt hung loosely from his bony shoulders. The new jeans he wore were cinched so tightly by his old belt with the familiar silver buckle that they ballooned out below the waist. He was moving so slowly and seemed so unsure of himself.

Last time we visited, I'd watched him in the sheep corral, roping a sheep for the dinner we didn't stay to eat. He was quick and strong, cornering the sheep, readying the rope without taking his eyes from the target, laughing when he missed the first throw. That was it! The laughter was missing, the sparkle in his eyes, the flash of white teeth, the joy. It finally hit me that Grandpa really was sick.

**28**

I guess my folks had the same thoughts. Finally they moved over to him.

"Dad," my father said, shaking his hand, "we're glad you're here."

"*Ya´at´eeh, Shiyé´.*"

"*Ya´at´eeh, Shizhe´e,*" Mom said, going from a handshake into a hug. She kept talking to him in Navajo, and he answered her, probably stuff about his trip and the family down home.

In a minute they stopped talking and turned to me.

"Brandon?" Mom said.

"Hi, Grandpa." I shook his hand.

"*Ya´at´eeh, Sitsuie,*" he said. Then he pulled me to him and gave me a hug. He was so much smaller than I remembered him. I felt like I could pick him right up and carry him to the car. He held my face against his chest for what seemed like half an hour. Just like Dad had said, he smelled like an Indian all right. I knew my father would roll down the windows on the way home.

After he released me from his death grip and I caught my breath, I thought I'd better try to start a conversation. I've never had much to say around my grandfather. For one thing, he always forgets and talks Navajo to me, which makes me feel like a dope because I don't know what he's talking about.

"So, how was your trip?" I asked.

"*Nizhoni,*" he said.

"Fine," Mom said quietly.

"Did you sit by any foxy chicks?"

It was a joke, but I guess he didn't get it. He looked at my mother for a translation, but she was at a loss, too.

At last Dad said, "Let's get your luggage." He pointed at the suitcases being pulled from the side of the bus.

"There's three," Grandpa said, pointing.

I could have picked two of them out. They were apple boxes tied up with rope. The tying was pretty ingenious because a loose loop of rope was left at the top of each box to use as a handle. I never would have recognized his third piece of luggage, a doll case. It was white plastic with pink writing and pictures of fashion dolls in all kinds of clothes and poses. When he pointed it out, I thought he was just making fun of it, so I laughed a little. Then Mom interpreted the Navajo he was saying.

"That white-and-pink one is his, Brandon."

"A doll case?"

"It contains all his personal stuff. Be careful with it."

"You go ahead and take that one," I said, but she already had Grandpa's arm and was walking him to the door.

My dad followed them, carrying the apple boxes, and I was left staring at the doll case. I couldn't very well leave it there, so I picked it up and hurried through the terminal, knowing that every person's gaze followed the kid in the black sweatshirt with the doll case clutched to his chest. I was trying to hide it, but I realized later that it probably looked like I was guarding it with my life.

In the car, my father rolled his window down a little and said, "Do you want something to eat, Dad?"

"*Hagoshii,*" Grandpa said.

"We'll just stop somewhere on the way," Dad went on. "It will be faster."

He slowed down and signaled to turn into a McDonald's stand.

"Maybe Dad wants to go someplace where we can go in and sit down. He's been on that bus all night," Mom said.

"Is a hamburger all right, Dad?"

"*Hagoshii,*" my grandfather said again.

"He doesn't want a bunch of people staring at him," Dad said. "It's more private in the car."

"More private for whom?" Mom said, and looked out her window while my father parked the car.

"What does everybody want? Never mind, I'll surprise you." My dad was out of the car before Mom and I had a chance to catch our breaths. He was either showing off by being the Doer for a change, or he didn't want to sit in the car with Grandpa while somebody else went to get the food.

Mom talked with Grandpa in Navajo for a while, then it was quiet.

"Little Brandon, all grown up," my grandfather said, and ruffled my hair. "You still in school?"

"Just for two more weeks."

It was kind of uncomfortable, trying to think of things to talk about.

"How're your sheep doing?" I finally asked.

Grandpa looked down at his hands, rubbing them slowly together. "Herman Talker is herding sheep. He's very lazy. Probably the sheep will get skinny before I get back to them."

Then it got quiet again.

"Mom, what does *hagoshii* mean?" I asked, because Grandpa used it so much.

"It means 'all right' or 'that's OK with me' or 'if that's what you want, I'll go along with it.' All sorts of things like that. It's a very versatile word."

My dad came back with hamburgers and fries for everyone, coffee for Grandpa, and soda pop for the rest of us. We ate in silence and then drove home.

31

= Pit        +64612

"Well, here we are," Dad said as we pulled into the driveway. "We're going to fix up a place so you can have your own room, but for now you're staying with Brandon in his room."

"That's good" was all Grandpa said.

He wasn't in any hurry to get inside. While Dad and I took his boxes and case to my room, Grandpa stood outside looking at our yard. He walked around slowly, looking at the plants, examining the thermometer on the side of the house, the hummingbird feeder. My mother stood by the car, watching him but not talking.

In a few minutes my dad said, "Brandon, go out and bring your grandfather in. Let him see his room and get used to the house."

"I think he likes it outside."

"Just go see if he's ready to come in. The neighbors probably wonder what's wrong with him, wandering around out there with nothing to do."

"I think the neighbors are too busy to worry about what Grandpa's doing," I said.

"Don't argue, just go bring him in here."

"*Hagoshii*," I said. My dad looked surprised, then he rolled his eyes toward the ceiling.

I hoped he knew that I was saying the *hagoshii* that means, "If that's what you want, I'll go along with it."

# Chapter Four

"The drawers on this side are yours, Grandpa," I told him. His head was still spinning from the tour of the rest of the house, the family room, living room, den, my parents' bedroom. He kept saying, "Three bathrooms."

"And this side of the closet is yours. Do you want me to help you unpack your stuff?"

*"Nidaaga, Shiyazhi."* He shook his head. "I'm not staying so long." He untied the ropes on his apple boxes and carefully coiled them up, putting them in a corner of the top drawer. "If I take everything from my boxes, your father will think I've made up my mind to make this my home. I have a home. I'll be going back soon."

"Whatever you say."

Apple boxes are really two boxes: one box fits over the top of the other box, and he had a little trouble slipping the top box off. When it was finally off, I saw shirts and jeans neatly folded. The Indian smell rolled

33

toward me. I tried to figure out what kind of a smell it was. It wasn't dirty like sweat or anything, just different.

"You know, it's not so bad living here. We have a TV, Mom's a pretty good cook, the mall is just a few blocks away with plenty of stores and a game room." I pulled myself up to sit on the top bunk. "You might get to like it."

He just looked over at me and smiled sadly.

"Until you're feeling better, anyway."

My father came in. "Getting settled?"

He opened the window. "How about a shower, Dad, or a bath to help you relax? Then a nap might catch you up on the sleep you missed on the bus."

Grandpa said something in Navajo.

"She's outside, in the back. She has this rose garden that keeps her pretty busy."

Dad noticed the boxes. "Brandon, why don't you help Grandpa get unpacked and settled in?"

"He doesn't want to yet."

"Well, we can't have boxes spread all over the room." He looked around nervously. "Maybe your mom's right, we ought to take these posters down, son. We don't want to give your grandfather nightmares."

Grandpa said some more in Navajo.

"They're singers, Dad. *Hataathlii.*"

Grandpa's turn.

"No, not that kind of singer. Making music with guitars and a keyboard . . . drums." Dad gave up. "You'll have to play some Van Halen for him," he said to me. "The word *singer* in Navajo means a medicine man, the man who sings the chants for healing and all that."

My grandfather made a long speech in Navajo and

34

laughed. Dad smiled. "He said that those guys look like they have very powerful medicine, so powerful that they have to wear chains to keep it in."

"He's just kidding, right?"

"Of course. Your grandfather has a great sense of humor."

He turned toward the door. "If you want to clean up, Dad, Helen left clean towels in the bathroom. Brandon, show him where the dirty-clothes hamper is; we ought to get these clothes washed."

As my father left the room, Grandpa looked at my rock poster once more. *"Hataathlii,"* he said, and chuckled to himself.

I put Grandpa's things in the closet while he sat on the bed and hummed quietly to himself.

"Your mother's outside?" he asked at last.

"Do you want to go out and see what she's doing? She spends a lot of time with her flowers. She loves to work outside."

He stood up, and I took him out back.

"Well, look who just can't get enough of the outdoors all of a sudden," Mom said with a smile as we joined her.

"I told Grandpa about your roses."

*"Nizhoni,"* Grandpa said. "That means 'beautiful.' "

*"Nizhoni,"* I said.

"Are you learning Navajo?" Mom asked me.

"Are you kidding! I know *hagoshii, hataathlii,* and *nizhoni.* Somehow I don't think that vocabulary will get me very far in a conversation on the reservation."

"The easiest way to learn a new language is to relax. Just listen to your grandfather all the time he's visiting and pretty soon you'll start understanding what's being said."

"I'm busy filling my brains with algebra and English and history, Mom. I don't have time—or room—for Navajo."

"You never know. You just might surprise yourself," Mom said.

My dad called me from the patio door. "Brandon, you're wanted on the phone."

As I passed him, he said, "It's David. What are they doing out there?"

"Planning where to build the hogan."

"Smart aleck!" Dad said.

"Why don't you go out and see?"

"Maybe later."

I picked up the receiver. *"Nizhoni,"* I said.

"Brandon?"

"It's me, the great speaker of Navajo."

"Very impressive, Cochise. What did you say?"

"I think I said, 'Beautiful.' "

"Thank you very much for the compliment. What else can you say?"

" 'Singer' and 'It's OK with me.' "

"You just might be able to work that into a conversation with Madonna."

"Thanks, but no thanks."

"So . . . how is it? Are you going to like rooming with your grandfather?"

"I don't know if I'm going to get a chance to find out. Grandpa insists that he's heading home with the next wagon train."

"Sounds like you're taking it personally."

"I just wish I hadn't spent all that time cleaning out

**36**

drawers for him. He doesn't even want to unpack his stuff." I laughed.

"I definitely hear hurt feelings in that laugh."

"I just don't know what to say to him, how to talk to him so he feels more comfortable around here."

"Give him some time. He'll settle in."

"Maybe . . . if I tie him up so he hangs around long enough to find out what a terrific roommate I am."

Ham laughed. "At least your modesty might win him over."

"Are you coming to meet him?"

"That's why I called. Are you sure it will be OK? Maybe I ought to give you guys a couple of days to adjust to the new living arrangements before barging in?"

"Come over now. I need some moral support. Besides, Grandpa might as well start meeting my seedy friends."

"I'll try to live up to that terrific introduction. It'll take me about fifteen minutes to take out the garbage and find my Indian beaded belt."

"Dressing up?"

"Just trying to make your grandpa feel at home."

"Forget it, Ham. That belt was made by Koreans, not Navajos. My grandfather doesn't notice things like that anyway."

"In that case, I'll be over in ten minutes."

Grandpa was still outside when Ham got here. We sat around my room for a while, listening to the stereo and talking about regular stuff.

"Tell me the truth, does it smell funny in here?" I asked after a few minutes.

"Funny?"

"You know, kind of Indian?"

Ham chuckled. "Just what does *Indian* smell like?"

"I can't quite identify what it is. All I know is my dad rolled down the window in the car and then came in here and opened my window. I think I can smell a peculiar aroma, but it might be my imagination."

Ham sniffed around my room a little.

"Dad even suggested that Grandpa take a bath and have his clothes washed."

"Your father is wasting his talents in engineering. He should be driving a Welcome Wagon."

Ham stuck his head in the closet. "The smell is stronger in here. What's in these boxes?"

"That's Grandpa's set of matched luggage. The stuff he won't unpack."

Ham sniffed the clothes. "That's it!" he said. "That smell is smoke. Not a bad smell, like stale cigarettes, but a nature-kind of smell. Like leaves burning in the fall, but a little sweeter."

I joined him in the closet, sniffing Grandpa's clothes. "It's cedar smoke. That's the kind of wood they burn down on the reservation. I recognize it now. I bought some cedar incense in a curio shop on one of our trips to the rez." I sniffed again. "Once you know what it is, it doesn't smell too bad."

"I like it."

"I'm going to tell my dad. Maybe he'll stop trying to herd Grandpa into the shower."

Ham laughed. "I wouldn't count on it."

He noticed the doll case and looked up at me. "Taking up a new hobby?"

"It's not what you think." I laughed. "Grandpa has his personal stuff in there. He must have taken it from one of the cousins down in Little Water. You've got to admit, it has kind of a special look about it.''

"Definitely.''

Grandpa came in right then and found us sitting in the closet with his boxes. We scrambled up.

"Grandpa, this is my best friend, David Berger.''

"How do you do, sir,'' Ham said, shaking my grand-father's hand.

"OK,'' Grandpa said.

It was quiet for a few minutes.

"How do you like the city so far, Mr. Rogers?'' Ham said.

I'd never told the fascinating name-changing story to Ham, so he didn't know that Grandpa was a Redhouse, not a Rogers. Grandpa just smiled. "I like it fine. I'm not staying very long though. I need to get home. I have things to do down there.''

"What's it like . . . the reservation, I mean?''

Grandpa sat on his bunk and rested his chin in the palms of his hands. "It's dry. It's quiet and there's lots of room, lots of sandstone and sagebrush and cedar trees.''

"Do you have a TV?''

Ham was really getting into this, which was pretty nice since I was the one who was supposed to make Grandpa feel at home.

"No TV. No electricity. Not three bathrooms, just one—a little house outside. My son-in-law, Stanley, takes my water barrels to the windmill once a week, on Saturday.''

"Sounds kind of rough,'' Ham said.

"It's OK, simple.''

"Grandpa lives in a house,'' I put in. "It's not one of

those round mud-and-log hogans that you see in the encyclopedia. It's a real frame house with stucco on the outside.''

"The door faces east,'' Grandpa said, ''like a hogan. The door should face east, that's the right way.''

I did a quick inventory of our house. "Our door, the one that goes into the garage, faces east,'' I said defensively.

No response from my grandfather.

"Maybe you'll get used to living up here,'' Ham said. "Maybe you'll find out you really like it.''

Grandpa smiled. "I must go back home as soon as I can. They need me down there.''

He stood up, went to the closet, and dug around in his boxes. He came out with a handful of clothes. "I'm going to take a bath now.'' He smiled at me. "So your father can relax.''

"It was nice to meet you, Mr. Rogers.'' Ham stood up.

"You don't need to call me Mr. Rogers. That's my son. You can call me Tom or *Shinali*,'' Grandpa said. "That's what Brandon is going to call me. It means 'grandfather' in Navajo. You and Brandon are best friends, like brothers. I can be Grandpa to both of you.''

"All right, *Shinali*. I'll talk to you later.''

"If I'm still here,'' he said, and went out.

"I think you're right about his not planning to stay too long,'' Ham said.

"He just might make it through dinner.''

Ham looked at his watch. "Speaking of dinner, I'm supposed to have the lawn mowed and edged by dinner. So I'll see you tomorrow . . . or talk to you on the phone, if something interesting develops. Right?''

**40**

"You'll be the first to know if we have an Indian uprising around here," I said.

Late that night, after a very quiet dinner and an evening of sitting around watching television and staring at each other, I lay on the top bunk trying to sleep. My grandfather was also trying to settle down. I felt the bed sway each time he rolled over. We had closed the window and the smoky "Indian" smell was strong, making me sorry I hadn't gone along with Dad's suggestion that we wash all of Grandpa's clothes while he was taking a shower. It was too late now. To get rid of that smell we'd have to wash all his bedding, too.

I tried the relaxation technique we'd learned in my gym class. Starting at my toes, I made my muscles loosen up. I concentrated on each muscle as my thoughts moved up my body—calves, knees, thighs. I was just getting to my buns and back when it started. At first it was so soft that I thought it might be my imagination. Concentration went down the tube as I listened harder. It was chanting! Just like my dad said, my grandfather chanted! Actually, it wasn't just like Dad had said, because it was very soft. It was soft and rhythmic and very boring!

I was going to suggest to Grandpa that he ought to try and get some sleep but decided to wait a minute and listen. Let him do his thing for a little longer, I thought. Next thing I knew, I was asleep.

# Chapter Five

It was still dark outside, and suddenly I was wide awake. I lay still, trying to figure out what woke me.

"Brandon," Grandpa whispered, and his rough hand shook my shoulder.

"What?" I said almost in panic.

"It's time."

"Time?"

"To run."

I sat up. "You mean run as in 'to walk real fast, to jog'?"

"If you get up early each morning and run to greet the sun, you'll always be healthy and quick."

"Are you crazy?!" I lay back down and rolled over to face the wall.

"I can see that your father hasn't taken much care in raising you, in teaching you the right way of things."

"He taught me that eight hours of sleep are essential for a growing boy," I mumbled into my blanket.

I felt the bed wiggle as Grandpa lay back down on his bunk. My heart was racing. Maybe getting scared to death gave my circulatory system just as good a workout as running would. My heart slowed down, but my eyes stayed open. All right, I'll humor him, I thought. He's only going to be here for a few days.

Turning, I leaned over the edge of my bunk. "Grandpa?"

"Mmmm?"

"Are you going to run, too?"

He stood up. I could see his white smile in the dim, early morning light. "It's you who's crazy," he said. "I'm too old."

"It figures." I threw back my covers.

"But I'll go with you to start you out." He already had his clothes on; maybe he slept in them. I hadn't noticed last night. "I'll make sure you run in the right direction."

"Thanks, but I think I can figure that out."

"You know where the sun comes up?"

I hadn't seen a sunrise come up for a long time. "I think so."

"Let's go find out."

I dressed in a hurry, and we went quietly through the dark house and into the gray of morning. It was cold. Even though it was May, the early morning air was like February.

"When do I start?" I asked as we stepped onto the sidewalk.

"Now," Grandpa said. "See the light sky above those trees? Run in that direction. Run till the sun appears above the earth, then run back."

**44**

"What are you going to do while I'm doing all the work?"

"Pray," Grandpa said simply.

"I'll trade you jobs."

"You're late, *Sitsuie*. Run."

I started off at an easy lope. "Race the sun!" I heard him call softly before I reached the corner.

I ran for another block, then stopped to look at the sky. The old sun was in no hurry to rise. I walked for another block, then sat down on a bench at the bus stop to rest for a few minutes.

The sun finally peeked above the trees, so I started back. I set a pretty good pace so I was sweaty and winded by the time I reached my grandfather.

"What a great idea for Sunday morning," I puffed.

"That's good for the first time." Grandpa smiled. "Tomorrow you'll do better."

"Tomorrow! You want me to do this again?"

"The right way is to do it every day." He grinned at the stricken look on my face. "And tomorrow you must run the whole way so that you can greet the sun with pride."

I bent down and tied my shoe, even though it didn't need it. "How did you know?"

"I know many things, because I'm in harmony with the world."

I grinned. Pretty smart, *Shinali*, I thought. You were just guessing and like a dope I opened my mouth and confirmed your suspicions.

"Let's go get my dad and mom up," I said. "They should be sharing this unique early morning experience."

"I have prayers to finish. You go ahead. I'll come in later."

I went to the kitchen and drank a gallon or two of water, wishing that in some strange, mystical way my parents would sense that I needed to talk to them and wake up. I wanted to discuss Grandpa's early morning expectations while the marathon was still fresh in my mind.

Since my mom and dad aren't really programmed for psychic manifestations, I filled the teakettle with fresh water and put it on the stove. Maybe I could transform the house into one of those coffee commercials on TV. The minute boiling water hit the instant coffee in their cups, my folks would drowsily pull back the covers, sniff the mountain-grown aroma, and smile.

When the kettle started whistling, I hurried to take it off. Then I remembered how soundly my dad sleeps. Aroma by itself probably wouldn't do the trick. I put the kettle back on the burner and let it shriek for a minute or two. No sign of life from the master bedroom.

I filled the cups and watched the fragrant steam float upward, fanning it toward the hallway. Still no response.

I'd just have to add a few more aromas. I pulled the package of bacon from the fridge, tossed it on the counter, and reached for a frying pan in the cupboard below the counter. It was on the bottom of the stack, and I tried to hold the other pans quiet while I slid it out. The top pan tipped and rolled onto my arms, and I clamped it against my chest to keep it from clattering to the floor.

As I set it on the counter, it dawned on me that I was defeating my get-Helen-and-Keith-out-of-bed strategy. I put the pan back, wobbled the stack until it slipped off again, and dodged back, letting it crash onto the linoleum. The sound was loud but not very long, so I gave the pan a kick. It made a satisfying racket scooting across the floor and banging against the leg of the table. Then I struggled as noisily as I could to free the frying pan. By the time I slammed it onto the burner of the stove, my mother was at the door.

"What's going on?" she asked sleepily.

"Did I wake you up?" I started peeling bacon strips and dropping them into the pan. "Sorry. I thought I'd get breakfast."

My dad staggered into the room, rubbing his face with both hands. "Do you know what time it is?"

"Exactly 5:52 A.M.," I said cheerfully. "I've been up for at least forty-five minutes."

"You have?" Mom's eyes widened just a fraction of an inch.

"I couldn't sleep."

Mom made her rumpled face take on a concerned expression. "Is something bothering you?"

"It's Grandpa."

She started toward my bedroom. "Is he sick?"

"He's fine," I said, and she turned back, walked over, and sat at the table. "At least he's fine physically."

Dad joined her, and I took their cups of coffee to them.

"I couldn't sleep because Grandpa was shaking me and telling me it was time to race toward the sun."

"Did you race?" Mom spooned sugar into her cup.

"I did . . . well, I didn't exactly *race*. I just sort of ran and walked and . . . sat for a little while."

"So the sun won," my dad said, picking up his coffee and blowing on it. My mother smiled.

"The point is," I went on, "I'm glad Grandpa's here and everything. I want him to feel welcome. I'm just

**47**

not sure I want to roll out of bed every morning at five o'clock, and that's what he has in mind.'' The bacon was beginning to curl a little, so I started rearranging the pattern of strips covering the bottom of the pan. ''I don't even mind running. I just wish he'd schedule it a little later in the day.''

Mom stopped in mid-sip. ''It's a little hard to delay the sunrise.''

I glanced back at her.

''I'll talk to him,'' Mom said. ''I'll explain that his grandson has led a somewhat pampered life. He's going to have to ease you into the challenge of Navajo tradition gently, a little at a time.''

''Maybe you can race the moon.'' Dad laughed and I knew I'd pulled him out of bed too early.

''Very funny,'' I said sarcastically, but I grinned because it was a pretty good crack for six o'clock in the morning.

''We're just teasing you, Brandon,'' Mom said. ''We know it's a little disruptive to share your bedroom with Grandpa. I really will talk to him about the running. It's probably a good idea for him to start sleeping in a little later anyway.''

They took simultaneous slurps of coffee.

''Where is your grandfather?'' Dad asked.

''He's out in the backyard, saying his prayers,'' I said, turning the bacon slices.

Mom stood up. ''I'll fry some eggs.''

''I'll go wash up,'' my father said, taking his coffee with him.

I made toast and set the table while Mom cooked eggs.

''I guess we're ready. I'll call your grandfather,'' she

**48**

said, moving to the door. I heard her talking in Navajo on the patio and Grandpa's voice answering. She laughed and he laughed. They were both smiling when they came in.

"Your grandfather says you might make a good Navajo yet," Mom said.

"If he doesn't kill me first."

A crazy idea kept nagging me—if I felt so good after *cheating* on the race, how would I feel if I really ran, if I did things the way Grandpa wanted me to?

Ham came over about eleven.

"I was going to sneak in and use a little cold water to wake you up," he said.

"Not a chance. I've been up since five."

"You're kidding!"

We were hanging around the family room watching baseball on television because Grandpa was taking a nap in my bedroom, our bedroom.

"How about a challenge, Ham old man?"

"A challenge?"

"There's this terrific Navajo custom of getting up before dawn every morning and racing toward the rising sun."

Ham laughed. "That's what you were doing at five o'clock this morning?"

I nodded.

"You could be arrested for running around this neighborhood at that hour."

"That's a good reason to give it up. Remind me to tell my grandfather; maybe he'll call off tomorrow's race."

"You mean he expects you to make this ancient custom part of your everyday soft and citified life?"

"Unfortunately." I nodded again. "Do you want to join me?"

"No way, Cochise! I have very definite priorities for my regularly scheduled activities, and sleep is at the top of the list."

"I guess some of us need more beauty sleep than others," I said, and he slugged me in the arm. "No kidding, Ham. I hate to admit it, but I feel so good."

"Because you ran a little ways this morning?"

"It isn't the physical exercise that gives me this high . . . and I'm not sure how I'll feel about it tomorrow morning, but just the fact that I had the discipline to do it makes me feel terrific about myself!"

"Careful, Cochise," Ham said. "This strange attitude is about to eliminate you from UGA." He did the UGA sign, and I repeated it.

We watched the game for a few minutes. Then Ham said, "Tell you what, O Great Runner to the Sun, if you maintain this ritual for two whole weeks—no slacking off, not even missing one morning—I'll join you the next week, when school's out."

"It's a deal," I said, and we shook hands.

I went and got Cokes and chips to make the baseball game a little more interesting.

"Is your grandfather still anxious to leave?"

My mouth was full of potato chips, so I just shrugged.

"If he leaves this week, there goes your old running program."

"Not necessarily. I can continue on my own."

Ham chuckled. "Sure you can, Mr. Self-discipline."

50

He took a swig of soda. "I, for one, think you need your genuine Navajo alarm clock."

I had to laugh.

"You seem a little more relaxed with your roommate today."

I shrugged. "I'm still not crazy about sharing my room, but I can stand it until Dad moves out of the den."

I should never have been so optimistic about getting along with Grandpa. Late that night, I woke up to familiar, quiet chanting.

"Grandpa?" I said.

No response.

*"Shinali!"*

The noise stopped.

"We've got to reach some agreement about all this praying you do."

"I'm not praying," Grandpa said. "I'm singing."

"Singing, praying—it all sounds the same to me, and it's driving me nuts."

The bed trembled as he rolled over and sat up. "I'm singing of home . . . of the little goats and how they lie down under a sagebrush and might get left behind. A herder must be careful and watch after them."

I sighed. "I need to get some sleep."

"When I sing, it makes me ready for sleep."

When you sing, it makes me ready for a mental ward, I thought, rolling over to lean down and talk to him. "How about singing it just once more and then calling it quits?"

"Quits?"

"You know, stop singing and go to sleep."

"If you listen, you'll be ready for sleep, too."

"I don't know about that, Grandpa."

"Listen for these words and you will know what the song says: *kl'izi yazhi*—that's a little goat—and *ts'ah*—that's a sagebrush—and *na'nithkaadi*—that's the sheepherder. Say the words with me."

I repeated the vocabulary with him a couple of times until I could say the words myself.

"Are you trying to make me learn Navajo?" I asked.

"It's a difficult language. People must learn it from birth."

"What about all the traditional stuff, the legends and stories that Dad says you know—are you going to tell me all that?"

"There isn't time."

"I mean, if you decide to stay here."

He laughed quietly. "There still isn't time."

The room was silent while I tried to figure out what he meant. Maybe there were so many legends that it took a lifetime to learn them all.

"I'm going to teach you only the important things," Grandpa interrupted my thought. "Language and legends you can learn on your own. Those things are in books. What I want you to learn is inside of me, in my heart."

"Oh" was all I could think to say.

"Are you ready for the song?" he asked.

"Go ahead."

"Should I sing?"

"Yes! Sing!" I was feeling less and less ready for sleep.

He started the song very softly, and I strained to hear

the words he'd taught me. It's funny, but I was disappointed when he stopped.

After a minute of silence, Grandpa said, "Should I sing it again?"

"Go ahead," I said. "But only a couple of times or we won't be able to get up and race the sun tomorrow."

"Your mother said you didn't want to race anymore."

"I'll try it once more . . . if I get enough sleep."

The room was silent for a minute.

"Grandpa?" I whispered.

"Mmmm?"

"I'm going to really race tomorrow . . . run the whole way."

"I thought you would," he said, and started singing the little-goat song softly.

# Chapter Six

The next morning I got up as soon as Grandpa said my name. I ran the whole time till the sun peeked over the trees, but I had to walk part of the way back. Grandpa told me that was OK, as long as I really tried to race the sun's rising.

Mom had breakfast ready and my father actually put down the morning paper when we sat down to eat.

"Well, who won the race?" he kidded.

"I did."

"How can you tell?"

"I got farther this morning than I did yesterday and I didn't stop running, so I figure I won."

"I think I'd like to hear the sun's side of the story."

As I poked a piece of toast into the yolk of my fried egg, I said, "You ought to join me."

Dad didn't laugh or protest, he just looked at me.

"Early in the morning, everything is so quiet, kind of clean and crisp. You get warmed up and breathing hard and just when your legs and arms get too heavy to lift one more time, a beam of sunlight streaks over the top of the horizon toward you and you get this feeling, like you could run for a million miles.''

Dad was holding his fork halfway to his mouth, listening. "I know that feeling," he said.

"You do?"

"I used to race the sun when I was a kid, you know."

Grandpa had been eating steadily while we talked. Now he said something to my father in Navajo.

Dad answered him . . . in Navajo.

Then Grandpa said something and Dad said something and all of a sudden they were talking to each other. The conversation ended in a laugh.

"Well?" I asked.

Dad looked at me. "Your grandfather was reminding me of the time I tried to cop out on a morning run. I ducked down behind a cedar tree to wait for the sun to come up. I didn't notice a yucca plant behind me, and as I crouched down, I sat right on one of its sharp spines. Needless to say, the yucca spike sent me straight up into the air and back into the race."

Everybody started laughing.

Dad went on, "The worst part was that I didn't know my father had seen my high-jump performance. When I got home, the family was all sitting around eating breakfast, like we are now, and Dad started laughing. He wasn't going to say anything, but he couldn't stop laughing, so the rest of the family pried the story out of him. At first I was so embarrassed that I just ducked my head. Finally I couldn't help joining in and laughing at the joke.''

We ate in silence for a minute.

"I hadn't thought of that in ages," Dad said.

I finished and took my plate to the sink. "Well? Do you want to get back in the race tomorrow?"

"No thanks," Dad said.

"There's not a single dangerous yucca plant along the route."

He smiled. "I have racquetball at the university rec center to keep me in shape now."

"It's kind of funny that Navajos knew all about keeping healthy before this current American craze of exercise came along."

"The Navajo aren't the only ethnic group to have traditions that promote healthy lives, Brandon."

"Yeah, but . . . here you are, raised Indian and getting a head start on an exercise program. Your Navajo traditions kind of—"

"You're going to be late for school," Dad interrupted.

"I just meant—"

"I know what you meant, Brandon. Just hustle or David will go on without you."

I hurried to brush my teeth. When I left the bathroom to pick up the books in my room, I almost crashed into my father.

"I'm sorry about cutting you short, Brandon. I know what you were saying," Dad said. "I'm not ashamed of being raised Navajo, son. I just prefer racquetball to presunrise jogging. You know what I mean?"

"Sure, Dad," I said. "To each his own, and all that stuff. I've got to get going. See you tonight."

"Right," he said, and went into the den.

I rushed through the kitchen, giving Mom her daily kiss. I know I'm too old for that, but we have this agreement. She gets one kiss a day, as long as no one's around to see me acting like a little kid.

"See you after school, Grandpa."

"We might still be at the doctor's when you get home," Mom said. "Just so you'll know."

"Who's sick?" I said before thinking.

My mother's expression told me I'd stuck my foot in my mouth. "Just a checkup for your grandfather."

"Right," I said, heading for the door. "Try to stay out of trouble, you two."

I hurried to meet Ham, who was standing at the corner, looking at his watch.

"For somebody who races with the sun," he said, grinning, "you're pretty late."

"Let's go. I'll tell you about my busy morning on the way."


When I got home after school, Mom and Grandpa were in the backyard. Mom was carefully spraying her roses to protect them from bugs. Grandpa was in the flower bed at the far end of the yard, digging with a shovel.

"How was Grandpa's visit to the doctor?" I asked.

"Fine." She was concentrating on the sprayer, so I didn't bother her with more questions.

I walked down to check on my grandfather.

"What are you doing, Grandpa?"

"Your mother said we can plant down here." He turned a couple of shovelfuls of dirt. "I thought we'd put in seeds for beans and squash."

"Need any help?"

He handed me the shovel. After a few minutes, I wondered what I'd gotten myself into. It was hard work.

I leaned on the shovel and asked, "Shouldn't we pull out these old plants from last year, so the ground will be clear?"

"Just turn the old plants into the ground. They'll help the new plants to grow strong."

He took the shovel and started working the soil. After a couple more minutes, I could see he was winded.

"My turn," I said.

He watched me work. "We'll plant together. When I go back home, it'll be your job to take care of this ground, to care for the young plants and gather their food."

"Still anxious to go back to Little Water, huh?"

He didn't answer.

"You might as well stay here until the garden's growing good."

He smiled and shook his head.

"Mom makes a special dish with beans. It's real good."

He just stood there smiling for a moment. "It takes time for plants to grow, for beans and squash to come."

"Only a month, maybe two."

"Sometimes a month is a very long time." He didn't look unhappy, just serious, but a sad feeling swept through me. I worked furiously with the shovel for the next half hour and finished turning the whole garden plot.

"When are you going to plant?" I asked, wiping sweat from my face.

"Tomorrow, maybe. Your mother said she will get some seeds for us."

My mother was very impressed with the small garden. I had to agree that this was the hardest I'd ever worked in the yard before.

We went in to wash up and get a cold drink of water. The phone was ringing when I came out of the bathroom.

"Cochise," Ham said, "where have you been?"

"Working in the yard."

"You're kidding. Did your mom bribe you or threaten you?"

"I did it on my own." I could hear him gasp. "I was helping Grandpa get ready to plant a garden."

"UGA is doomed!"

I laughed.

"I called to tell you that Food World has Mrs. Morton's Chicken on sale. Can you get away for a little while?"

Mrs. Morton's Chicken is a very important tradition for Ham and me. His mother once sent him to Food World to buy ten packages each of frozen thighs, breasts, and drumsticks. She likes to keep plenty on hand in their deep freeze. When we got to the store, they had plenty of drumsticks and thighs, but only two packages of chicken breasts, so Ham asked Mr. Webster, the assistant manager, if they had any more stored somewhere. Webster is a nice old guy, always anxious to help. He got on the loudspeaker and said, "Louis, will you check in the back for Mrs. Morton's Breasts?" Ham and I really cracked up. Mr. Webster turned red and started sputtering into the speaker. It's a moment that will live in our memories forever.

Now, whenever they have Mrs. Morton's Chicken on sale, Ham and I go in, find Mr. Webster, and ask him if they have any chicken breasts in the back. The first few times we did it we hoped that he'd make his famous announcement over the PA, but he never did. He'd just take us over to the frozen-food case to check. There were always plenty of packages there. He doesn't check anymore, he just smiles sheepishly and turns red. I know teasing him like that won't get us into the Humanitarian Hall of Fame, but it's funny in a dopey way. Mr. Webster's a good sport and humors us. We all get a good laugh out of it.

"I'll ask," I said. In a minute I came back. "I can go. Be over in a minute."

"I'll be ready."

My mother came into my room just as I hung up the receiver.

"Why don't you take Grandpa with you and pick up the seeds he wants to plant?" she asked.

"Are you serious!"

"Why not?"

"Mom, Food World is at the mall."

"I know where the store is, Brandon." Her voice was developing a defensive edge.

"All my friends hang out at the mall, Mom. I don't want to be dragging my grandfather around down there. Nobody drags his grandfather around down there."

"Don't make a big deal out of this, Brandon. Grandpa just might like to get out for a change, see some of the stores."

I sat down on Grandpa's bunk. "I'll pick up the seeds for him."

"He'll feel more a part of the project if he helps in selecting the seeds."

"Then take him to the store tomorrow, Mom." I started counting my change, in case I wanted a candy bar or something. "Look, I'm not going to parade the

**61**

mall with him when all the kids from school are around to make wisecracks. That's all there is to it, Mom!''

I looked up and saw Grandpa at the door. I didn't know how long he'd been there. Mom followed my glance.

My grandfather looked at the floor.

"I've got to go," I said, pushing past Grandpa and running out the front door. Somehow, the trip to Food World didn't seem so much fun anymore.

# Chapter Seven

I wasn't very good company on the way to Food World, and finally Ham asked me what was wrong. I told him I was just tired from playing Farmer John. After we found Mr. Webster and he did his incredible blushing act, I felt a little better. In fact, I forgot all about being a creepy grandson. After all, I'd only agreed to share my room and help Grandpa feel welcome. I hadn't signed up to be his activities director.

Some kids from school were hanging around the plaza in the middle of the mall, and we stopped to check out what was going on. Ann and Marcey were sharing a piece of pizza. Greg Paulson was watching every bite and licking his lips. While we were talking, the girls had an overwhelming attack of generosity and gave him a piece of pepperoni off the top.

"Want a Coke?" Ham asked.

"Why not?"

"I'll get them." He disappeared into the line in front of Hamburger Heaven.

"Hey, catch the time traveler from frontier days," Greg said. I followed his gaze, and my heart started pounding its way into my stomach.

"One of your relatives has escaped from the barbed wire, Cochise," Ann said. She was making a joke, but it was true. My grandfather was wandering slowly down the mall. The bun at the back of his head hung loosely to one side, his shirttail stuck out, and he still had dust from our garden on his jeans and sneakers. It looked as if he hadn't even taken the time to wash up. He shuffled slowly between the shoppers, lost in his wonder of big-city life.

Don't let him see me! Please, don't let him see me, I thought. He was coming straight toward us.

"Let's go check out the game room." I jumped up.

"In a minute," Marcey said, leisurely finishing the last bite of pizza. "We'd better wait for Ham."

"He'll know where we went. Come on." I gave Greg's arm a pull and started looking for a crowd to get lost in.

Ham came up with the drinks, and I tried to keep his attention from my grandfather's direction.

"We're going to the game room," I said, pushing him in that direction.

"Hey, wait a minute, dope!" Some of the soda slopped out and ran down his arm. "Relax a minute and drink your Coke. They don't allow food in there."

"What's your hurry?" Marcey said, wadding up the paper plate from the pizza and tossing it on the floor.

I started off, hoping they'd follow. After a few steps, I turned to see if they were coming. As I looked across

64

the mall, my eyes met my grandfather's and then quickly focused on the floor.

At that moment Ham looked back, too.

"Hey, Brandon, there's your grandfather."

The other kids glanced over, recognized the "frontier-days time traveler," and turned to me.

"Hey, Tom," Ham was calling and waving. "Hey, *Shinali!*"

But Grandpa didn't acknowledge his greeting. He just continued to look at me.

"That's your grandfather?" Ann's voice was full of surprise. "Brandon, I'm really sorry. I was just . . ."

"Come on, you guys," I broke in. "We're wasting time. Let's go."

Before we went around the corner, I turned for one more look. Grandpa was picking up the wadded plate that Marcey had dropped. He walked over and put it in the trash.

I lost three quarters in Space Invaders, one right after another, before I finally gave up and told the other kids I had to get home.

"Let's go," Ham said.

"That's OK; you can stay."

"I'm ready to leave."

"If it's all right with you, Ham, I'd rather go by myself. I need to be alone for a little while."

He shrugged. "Trouble with your grandfather? Is that why he ignored us?"

"Not really trouble with him," I said. I felt as if I might start crying any second, so I turned and started toward the door. "Trouble with me," I said, but he probably didn't hear me.

As I weaved my way through the crowd to the mall

entrance, I felt kind of sick. Then I started feeling mad. Mad at my Grandpa for coming to the mall. Mad at my friends for being stupid and making cracks about him. Finally I realized that I was really mad at myself. Mad because I was starting to love my grandfather. Angry because I'd felt ashamed of him, because I'd pretended I didn't know him, that he didn't mean anything to me.

By the time I got home, my anger had grown into fury. I marched through the kitchen, down the hall—noting that Grandpa was lying on his bunk—and found my parents in their bedroom. The door was open and I barged right in. I slammed it behind me.

"How could you?" I said to my mother, not noticing her red, wet eyes, not seeing my dad's solemn expression.

She didn't talk, just answered with a surprised, puzzled look.

"How could you send Grandpa after me, have him follow me to the mall? I told you how I felt about that!"

"Brandon, I . . ."

"Well, the agreement's off! No more giving in . . . going out of my way to make Grandpa feel welcome. No more running in the morning or planting stupid bean seeds, or . . ." Even as I was saying it, I wasn't sure I meant it, but I couldn't stop myself. Anger just kept filling my throat and spilling out of my mouth. ". . . or singing stupid songs about little goats!"

The tears started coming and sobs mixed with the crazy words I was almost shouting at my parents. "I can't stand it anymore! I'm sick of sharing my room, of going to school smelling like an Indian!" Tears were diluting my anger quickly. "Just write to Aunt Ethel . . . tell her . . . just tell her that it's not working out."

I stopped talking and sank to the bed, letting tears drop

on the knees of my jeans, letting my nose run like a stupid little kid.

Mom walked over and put her hand on my shoulder, then sat next to me, her arm around me. I wanted to give in to the comfort of her hug, but I felt too awful. I didn't deserve any comfort. I'd said terrible things, stuff I didn't even mean, but how could I take them back?

Mom brushed her fingers through my hair. "Brandon, I know that things haven't been all that easy, that adjustments . . ."

I turned from her and shrugged her arm from my back.

My dad said, "Brandon, we can't send your grandfather back to Little Water." He stopped and rubbed his hands over his face. "I won't send him back. He needs to be here, where he can get the help, the comfort he needs."

My mom put her arm around me again. "At the doctor's office today . . ."

I jumped up. I had a terrible feeling about what she was going to say, and I couldn't stand to hear it. She seemed glad to stop, to try and find a better way to put it.

I looked from my dad's sad face to my mother's and back again. Before they could say any more, I ran out of their room, slamming the door for a second time. I stopped in the kitchen, wondering where to go, where to find the right kind of place to explore my thoughts, get my feelings back in perspective.

Finally I ran out the back door, to the far end of the yard, and sank to my knees, letting hot tears drop to the newly turned ground of the garden.

I'm not sure how long I sat there and cried. It wasn't

long, because the bottom of the sun was just touching the tops of the trees and the orange of sunset was filling the sky when I noticed my grandfather standing behind me.

"I have the seeds," he said, ignoring my dirty, tear-streaked face. "Perhaps there's time to plant them."

"OK." My voice was soft.

"Maybe just the squash today. Tomorrow, we can plant the beans. They take longer."

"OK."

I watched him work his hands through the soft soil and pull it into five mounds parallel to the back fence about four feet apart. While he worked he talked.

"I didn't follow you, you know. At least, I didn't follow you to be with you. I went to find a store, to buy the seeds. I know that I look out of place here . . . in your world, that people look at me with curious stares. I also knew that you wouldn't want me to talk to you when you were with your friends. You should have trusted me. I understand many things."

"I'm glad you understand it, Grandpa. I sure don't." I wanted to kneel down and help, but I was afraid I'd get in his way. "I don't know what was wrong with me. . . . I think I was afraid that those kids wouldn't really see you. They'd see the earrings and stuff but not the real you—the one I know."

His hard brown hands pushed and patted the soft earth.

"I understand your thoughts, but understanding doesn't make such thoughts right."

He turned his face toward me so I could see his smile. "This is one of those important things that I told you I would teach to you."

**68**

"Should I write it down?"

He laughed. "If you have to write it down, you haven't learned it."

He turned back to the work he was doing. "A person's family is the only thing that continues from one time to the next, from one person to the next. I am a mixture of all those that came before me and each day, I'm adding to myself. I passed myself on to your father . . . and now to you. Each day you add to that which you've been given and you will pass it on to your children. It has always been this way. To forget that upsets the balance of the earth."

Grandpa stood up and stretched his back muscles.

"Make a hole for the seeds in the top of each hill," he said. He walked back to the house and returned with a plastic gallon jug—an old milk container—from the trash. He'd filled it with water. Carefully he poured water into each hole I'd made. We waited while the water soaked into the dirt.

"Once, your father knew the importance of family," Grandpa went on, "but he has pushed it far back into his mind and hidden it behind other thoughts. He stays busy so that the things he once knew will stay buried, but he is not happy."

He took a package of seeds for yellow summer squash from his back pocket, tore it open, and handed it to me. "Put five seeds into each hill."

I did it while he continued to talk.

"Your father thinks I'm unhappy because he doesn't live on the land where he was born, because his life is more like the Whites' than the Navajo way. He thinks I am angry because he changed his name." He made a strange sound, almost a laugh. "He doesn't understand

**69**

that Keith Rogers and Kee Redhouse are the same man. A name doesn't make that much difference. He didn't need to change his name, but it doesn't matter so much that he did. What he can't change is the human being once named Kee and now called Keith.''

Grandfather covered the seeds and made a little basin at the top of each hill, like a pond. He poured water onto each mound. Then he stood up and again watched the earth absorb the water. He put a hand on my shoulder.

"Today, I wasn't sad for myself when you looked at me and didn't see me, didn't want your friends to know that we are part of one another. I felt bad for you, *Sitsuie*. To be ashamed of what you are or of the people you come from is a very sad thing.''

I turned and hugged him. "I'm not ashamed of you, *Shinali*. I love you,'' I said, smelling the soft tang of cedar smoke.

He didn't say any more, just patted my back.

In a few minutes my father came out. "Dinner will be ready in a minute.''

"The squash is planted,'' Grandpa said.

"The squash? Well, that's good, Dad. Maybe you two squash planters ought to wash up before we eat.''

Grandpa didn't say anything; he just went inside.

My dad cleared his throat. He always does that when he's nervous. "Brandon, about your grandfather staying here . . .''

"That's OK, Dad. I really don't mind. I was just blowing off steam because . . . because I didn't understand something.''

"I realize how hard it is. I mean, you have your grandfather right in that room with you, probably talking to you all the time, singing, telling you all those stories, reminiscing about reservation life . . ."

"It's OK, Dad. Really."

"And I hear what you're saying about the smell. Grandpa's been bathing, but I told your mom that we need to launder his bedding and clothes . . ."

I wished I could go back in time and change things, take back all I'd said in my parents' room.

"Look, Dad, I didn't mean all that stuff I said to you and Mom. I don't mind sharing my room with Grandpa. I'm even getting to like the smell of cedar smoke. Don't get all upset and start changing things just because I went a little crazy and shot off my mouth."

"I just want this arrangement to be as easy as possible for you, Bran. Even though it's temporary, I don't want it to disrupt your life a lot."

My dad put his arm around me and we walked back to the patio.

"We'd better go in," I said. "Mom probably has dinner ready."

"Just one more minute, son." Dad sat down on a patio chair and gestured toward the one next to him. I sat down. "Your grandfather really is very sick, Brandon. He has cancer of the pancreas. They tried to take him to the doctors down home but he's so stubborn, he wouldn't go. And now there's nothing we can do about it . . . just make him as comfortable as possible. That's why I can't send him back to Little Water. He needs people around to watch him, to help him, to make him happy."

A wave of grief swept through me, an overwhelming sense of loss and loneliness. But I had no more tears left

71

to shed. I just sat there and stared into the darkness of our yard.

"He was a good father, Brandon. He taught me so many things. He introduced me to hard work. Kind of like he's introducing you to it." Dad messed up my hair. "All the success I've had really came because of the foundation he gave me."

He rubbed his hands over his face for a few seconds.

"I've been away from him for so long," my dad went on, more to himself than to me, "that I hardly know how to talk to him, how to let him know how I feel."

"He'll know, Dad."

My father looked over at me.

"Grandpa knows lots of things. He's in touch with feelings and thoughts that lots of people don't even know they have. He'll know what we're thinking."

I don't know if my dad was relieved or if he thought what I said was ridiculous, but he smiled. Then he said, "Maybe you're right."

We went in and sat through a quiet meal. Every few minutes my mom would jump up to get some more bread or butter, or something else that we didn't need. When her back was turned, she would wipe her eyes.

# Chapter Eight

Grandpa woke me up again the next morning. I wasn't as excited to race as I'd been other mornings, but once I started, it turned out to be the best run yet. I ran all the way to meet the first ray of sunlight and then all the way back to *Shinali*.

"You were right, Grandpa," I puffed. "I feel terrific."

"It only works as long as you run every morning."

"I know; you told me. I'm going to keep running."

"Even when I'm no longer here to wake you?"

I looked up at him, then quickly away. "What are you talking about? You're going to be here to wake me."

He kept walking toward the backyard as I turned to the front door.

"You've got to wake me up," I called after him. "You're my genuine Navajo alarm clock."

I heard him laugh.

"Do you want company? Do you want me to come with you while you say your prayers?"

"No," he said without turning to look at me.

"So? What's the story?" Ham asked before I could even say good morning.

"Story?"

"What's going on between you and your grandfather, Cochise? He didn't look all that thrilled to claim you as one of the tribe last night at the mall."

Talk about getting things backward!

"Did Marcey and those guys tell you what I did?"

"A little bit. They weren't exactly shouting the story from the rooftops."

"They probably won't even talk to me today."

"*They* won't talk to *you*? Why's that?"

The good feeling I'd gotten from the morning's race was quickly disappearing beneath an ugly blanket of shame. Ham had a right to know what a jerk he had for a best friend.

I took a deep breath but Ham didn't let me start my explanation. "The way they told it," he said, "it's *you* who shouldn't be talking to *them!* Marcey said that they made fun of your grandfather and you tried to protect him by pushing everybody around and trying to get them out of there."

I had to laugh.

"The truth is, I was embarrassed. I didn't want those guys to know that the old man they were making fun of was my grandfather."

"You were ashamed of your own grandfather!" Ham stopped in the middle of the sidewalk and stared at me.

"Pretty creepy, aren't I?"

"Creepy isn't the word for it, Cochise."

The shame wrapped tighter around my chest. "I wish I could explain it, Ham. I know you'd understand."

"I already understand, Brandon. Creepy isn't the word—normal is the word for how you felt."

"Normal?"

"Everybody gets embarrassed about their grandparents." Ham was grinning. "And their parents . . . even brothers and sisters. I even get embarrassed about you, Cochise, and you're my best friend! If you think *your* grandfather is embarrassing, you ought to go someplace with *my* grandfather! He's the King of Embarrassment!"

"Does your grandfather wear his hair in a bun?"

"Worse. My grandfather *talks!*"

I looked over at him.

"Grandpa Berger is losing his hearing, so he doesn't just talk, he shouts. I accompanied him to the rest room at a movie once. That experience deserves an exclusive room in the Embarrassment Hall of Fame."

"I'm listening."

"Picture this: It's intermission, see, so everything is crowded. We walk into the mens' room and I get in one line and Grandpa gets into the line next to me. The guy in front of my grandfather is a young man with long blond hair. Good old Mr. Berger can't keep his thoughts to himself, he has to share them with everyone in the whole washroom, with every being in the whole universe. 'What's this?' my grandpa says. 'They're letting girls in the mens' lavatory these days?' He turns to me. 'Tell me, Davey, is this a girl here or maybe a boy without a quarter for a haircut?' "

I started laughing.

"I'm thinking that the guy might turn around and punch my grandfather right in the nose. As his loyal grandson, I'd be expected to defend him. Thank goodness the young guy's cool. He turns to my grandpa and

75

says, 'What's your problem, sir?' Grandpa says, 'Problem? I have no problem, young man.' The guy turns back; it's his turn at the urinal. 'It's you who has a problem, young man,' my grandfather continues. 'You're breaking your parents' hearts with hair like that.' The guy just laughs.''

By that time, I was laughing so hard I had to stop walking. Ham loves an audience. He just kept rolling.

"So the young guy steps over to the sink to wash his hands and my grandfather steps up to the urinal. Grandpa says, in his quiet voice, as quiet as a Boeing 747, 'He doesn't flush? What's this, the young man's arm is broken?' ''

It was a good thing that it was the last week of school and I didn't have books to carry. They would have ended up on the ground as I laughed.

When I finally stopped, I asked Ham, "Are you saying that you would have avoided your grandfather in the mall just like I did?"

Ham looked at me. "Never," he said. "Do I look like a creep?"

Then he grinned. "In the first place, my grandfather isn't as sensitive as yours. He wouldn't go along with being ignored, he'd have shouted at me, chasing me down the mall until everyone within a mile radius had their cameras out. In the second place, my grandfather is rich and, more important, a show-off. He'd insist on treating us all to pizza. A full stomach makes embarrassment so much easier to handle.''

We walked a little ways in silence.

"I guess I'm thinking that what you did isn't so strange, Brandon," Ham finally said. "Don't go feeling

**76**

guilty about it. As long as your grandfather knows that you care about him.''

''I do care about him.''

''I know. He knows it, too.''

''Do you really think he does?''

''Of course. If you didn't care about him, would you get up before dawn to run a crazy race just so he can have the honor of being timekeeper?''

After school, Ham insisted that we go to his house for a snack.

''Nobody is home, so we'll have free access to any number of wonderful taste sensations hidden around our kitchen,'' he said.

As it turned out, his kitchen had about the same taste sensations as mine does. We settled on peanut butter and jelly. Ham brought out a handful of little plastic containers of jelly—the kind you get with toast in restaurants. That's one of the fascinating things about the Berger house. Ham's dad is a salesman, and he's on the road a lot of the time. He's always bringing stuff like the jelly back with him. His family has sugar and diet sweetener in little paper packages and little bars of soap from motels in their bathroom. Mr. Berger brings home all the extra stuff from his trips, and Mrs. Berger hates to waste anything. When you eat soup at their house, your crackers come individually wrapped in cellophane.

''So, now what?'' Ham asked after we'd finished our snack. ''No homework. Want to watch TV?''

''I think I'd better be getting home. I told Grandpa that I'd help him plant beans today.''

''Beans today, squash yesterday, running races every

morning—this is positively my last warning! Uga, uga, uga,'' he said, and pulled the imaginary steam-whistle rope.

I repeated the sign, grinning.

"Thanks. I needed that. I was almost overwhelmed by the desire to participate in hard work." I headed for the door. "I promise to change my ways."

"Or suffer the consequences," Ham called after me. "Blisters, sweat stains, strained muscles . . ."

When I got home, my grandfather was in the backyard. He had most of the beans planted.

"I was going to help you," I told him.

"It's easy work."

I pulled the hose down to the end of the yard so he could water the rows he'd planted. I didn't want him to carry his old gallon jug back and forth from the house. Then I took the shovel around to the flower bed on the other side of the house under our bedroom window and started turning over the soil. I was pulling the soil into mounds by the time Grandpa came around to see what I was doing.

"I'm going to plant more squash," I explained. "I want to be able to look out the window and see how they're doing anytime I feel like it."

"You've got the ground ready, but this isn't a good place for squash."

"What's wrong with it?"

"It's just wrong. The sun warms this ground at the wrong time of the day."

"Let's just try it, Grandpa."

"*Hagoshii*," he said, and I wondered which meaning he intended. "We have lots of squash planted already."

"If the squash plants grow, we can sell squash to other people around here. Hardly anyone grows their own vegetables."

"Grow more than you need and sell the extra, that sounds like a White man's idea."

My head snapped up to look at him in hurt surprise.

"Not a bad idea," Grandpa said quickly. "If we raise lots of squash, we should share."

"We'll give some to Ham's family."

"Ham?"

"You know, David, my friend."

Grandpa nodded.

"You know, *Shinali*, when school's out I bet Ham will want to help us with this garden. Friday's the last day, and then we'll have all summer to water and weed and pick squash and beans . . . all that stuff."

Grandpa got very quiet. "Not all summer, *Shiyazhi*," he said at last. "Not all summer."

# Chapter Nine

Friday was the last day of school, a big waste of time. Kids have to show up for half a day so that the teachers can give one last lecture on working hard and developing our potential. Then the single teachers rush off to tour Europe and the married ones hurry to summer jobs at Safeway or J.C. Penney. Even though today was just as big a waste as other last days, I liked it. For one thing, it was the first time I'd seen Mr. Thompson smile all year. He'd been busy for the past nine months wrinkling his forehead in frustration as he tried to explain algebra to us. But today he was full of enthusiasm about a Math Camp he was going to teach for four weeks. I think he was trying to talk us into enrolling, but phrases like "the fascinating world of logic and numbers" and "an exciting discovery around every academic corner" didn't fool me. It was summer-school prison camp for the guys who couldn't con their math teachers into a passing grade.

"I'd die before going to Thompson's Math Camp," I told Ham on the way home.

"Me, too. I'll take the 'fantastic world of baseball and messing around' over logic and numbers any day."

We walked along in silence for a few minutes, contemplating the luxury of the long, lazy summer days stretching out before us.

"What *are* we going to do?" I finally asked. "We ought to plan at least a few things to fill up the summer."

"We're going to do what we've done every summer since we became best friends."

I waited to hear what that was.

"For the first two weeks, we're going to sleep in every morning." He looked over at me. "Except those who have been initiated into the Secret Order of the Racers to the Sun."

I laughed. "If I remember right, a new member is about to join the fraternity."

He ignored me. "Starting the third week, we slip quickly down the steep slope of boredom and spend the rest of the summer driving our folks crazy until they start petitioning the school board for year-round schools."

I laughed. Ham has an uncanny memory.

"Actually, there is one experience that every young man should have at least once in his lifetime." He stopped, turned to face me, and put his hand solemnly on my shoulder. "Your lucky day is coming up, Brandon Rogers."

Then he stood there, silent.

"Well? Describe this once-in-a-lifetime opportunity."

He grinned. "You know my grandfather? The one whose voice box is the marvel of medical science . . . and the Broadcasters of America?"

I nodded.

"We're taking him to the cemetery next Monday."

"You mean the cemetery doesn't pick up?"

"It's Memorial Day, dope. We're going to go put flowers on all my relatives' graves. What do you say, Cochise? Want to come along?"

Since I didn't have any relatives in cemeteries around here, Memorial Day was just another day to me. The only difference was that my dad got a day off to supervise the yard work.

"I think that's our get-the-yard-ready-for-summer day."

"Don't give me that excuse, Brandon. You and *Shinali* have been killing yourselves all this week, weeding and raking and doing all that yard-work stuff."

"I don't know, Ham. It seems like a pretty depressing pastime."

"It will be even more depressing if you don't go."

"It will?"

"Of course it will, because . . ." He threw himself to his knees and put his hands up in a pleading gesture. ". . . I'll kill myself if I have to go alone. Please . . . please . . . If you have a single ounce of humanity, you'll agree to come along."

I laughed. "I'll ask. If it's OK with the rest of my family, I'll come."

He jumped to his feet. "That's better. Anyway, you'll love what my grandpa does to a graveyard."

I gave him a puzzled glance.

"Ever hear of a 'voice that would wake the dead'?"

"I can hardly wait."

After I left Ham at the corner, an amazing thought hit me. During all that talk of cemeteries and death, the fact that my grandfather was very sick and probably dying had never connected. I've developed this uncanny ability to ignore things that I don't want to exist. I block them out of my mind, and they're no longer there to worry me. If some other guy's grandfather were really sick, he'd probably concentrate on that one thing and forget everything else. With me, I concentrate on everything else and forget that one terrible thing. It wasn't that I hadn't grown to love Grandpa. I'd grown to love him more than I'd intended. My mind refused to entertain the possibility that he wouldn't be around much longer.

He was in the yard, as usual, but he wasn't working. In the past week, I'd come to expect to find him slowly raking or kneeling at a flower bed with his hands busy in the soil. Today he was kneeling on the lawn, motionless. I noticed an envelope on the grass next to him. In one hand he clutched a piece of paper while his other hand held something to his face.

"I'm ready to work, *Shinali*," I said as I came up behind him.

He jumped in surprise, like I'd shaken him out of a daydream, and it was then I noticed he was crying. He wasn't sobbing or being noisy about it, but his cheeks were wet. As he lowered his hand from his face, I saw he was holding weeds.

"What are you doing?" I asked.

"*Ts´ah,*" he said, holding the weeds out to me. "Sagebrush. Your cousin Alex sent some to me."

"He sent you sagebrush?"

"Your mother wrote a letter home for me. I told her what I was thinking about and she wrote it down. It's easier for me to talk than to write now. I told them that I

**84**

missed the smell of the sage, the smell of the sheep corral and cedar smoke."

He held up the piece of paper. "My grandson wrote me a letter. He sent the sage."

He offered the twigs to me.

I took a couple of sniffs. The strong, tangy scent stung the inside of my nose.

"Pretty strong," I said, giving them back.

My grandfather sniffed again and closed his eyes. "When I smell sage, I can see myself young again, running up the wash from my mother's hogan, hiding from my brother behind the cedar tree, waiting with my heart pounding for him to reach the tree and run on past so I can jump up and call to him and mimic his surprised, angry expression that changes into laughter."

I sat down on the grass.

"I close my eyes and smell the sage and I'm home, feeling my way to the sheep corral with unsure feet in the dark. It's early spring and I'm checking for new lambs," Grandpa went on, "or I'm sitting on the crooked cedar tree near the woodpile, wiping sweat from my face, watching a hawk circle far above my head, growing smaller and smaller as he drifts on warm air without moving his wings."

He wasn't talking to me anymore. In fact, he'd forgotten I was even there, but I waited quietly and listened. His words were painting images in my mind. As he spoke, the scenes changed, the activities changed, but the love in his voice for the desolate old desert down there remained constant. We sat side by side sharing a lifetime of mind snapshots and home movies in just a few minutes.

Finally I noticed he was crying again.

85

"I must go home, *Sitsuie*," he said at last. "My mind returns home more and more often now, but that's not enough. I've got to take my body home. I've got to see these things with my eyes, not just my thoughts."

He reached out and clasped a thin brown hand on my shoulder. "I'm tired and homesick and if I don't go back soon, I will never see my home again."

"Come on, Grandpa. You know that you haven't been sleeping very well. You're just . . ."

He didn't seem to hear me. "You've got to help me convince your father to let me go back. I've tried to tell him, but he doesn't hear. He won't hear. He picks up a book or turns on the television. When his mind is so full of other things that what I say can't get in, he asks me if I've taken my pills."

He turned to look at me, and suddenly I knew that he was right. Maybe it was the loneliness in his dark eyes or the tear that slid quickly to his jaw that told me. I'm not sure why, but I knew that he had to go home.

"Let me talk to Dad. He doesn't always listen to me either, but I'll see what I can do."

Grandpa smiled and wiped his cheeks.

At dinner, I asked about going with the Bergers on Memorial Day.

"I thought we'd work in the yard," Dad said.

I smiled because I knew he had the day planned. For a guy who says he's nontraditional, my father is very set in his ways.

"I don't think you can find a day's worth of work to do out there, Keith," Mom said. "Your father and Brandon have been putting in long hours on the yard lately. You've been too busy to notice."

**86**

Dad had been disappearing into the den to develop final exams and grade term projects.

"Brandon has been working in the yard?" He sounded amazed.

Mom and Grandpa smiled.

"So? How about it? Do you want to get me out of your hair for an afternoon or not?"

"Who could say no when you put the offer so eloquently?" my dad said.

"Good. I'll go tell Ha—David," I said, and got up from the table.

I waited till Dad was relaxing alone in the family room with the newspaper before I approached him about Grandpa. I figured I could use the trusted strategy of "divide and conquer." While Mom was loading the diswasher and straightening the kitchen, I could tell my father that *she* thought taking Grandpa home for a visit was a good idea. Later, I'd find Mom alone and tell her that *Dad* thought it was a good idea. As long as they didn't talk to each other until after I'd talked to each one of them, they'd think that the other one had come up with a great idea.

"Dad?"

He made an almost-interested sound from behind the newspaper.

"What do you think about going down to Little Water for a visit the week before summer quarter starts? Grandpa can check on things down there and Aunt Ethel and those other guys can check on Grandpa."

Dad lowered the newspaper and looked at me. "Did your mother put you up to this?"

"Mom? No!" I stammered in surprise. "It's just an

**87**

idea I had on my own. Mom thinks it's a good plan, though," I finished, collecting my thoughts.

"I'll bet she does." He lifted the paper back up. "She already brought it up. I told her I couldn't work it out."

He turned the page and snapped the newspaper to straighten it. "I have a new class to teach next quarter and I'm just starting to put the syllabus for it together. I also have an article almost ready for *Engineering*. That week's just too important to be wasting it down on the reservation."

"How about just going down one day, visiting one day, and coming home the next?"

He dropped the paper again. "No, son. Maybe we can fit a trip in at the end of summer quarter. There's a longer break between quarters then."

He brought the paper between us again.

"That's going to be too late! We need to go down there right away!"

Dad threw the paper to the floor and stood up. "Damn it, Brandon! I said no and that's exactly what I meant. Your grandfather's too sick to spend eight hours in a car, and I can't afford to take all that time to chauffeur him around. I'd appreciate it if you and your mother would try and understand that and stop the nagging! Any questions?"

I just looked at him for a few seconds, and then he walked past me and into the den, slamming the door.

When Mom came in, her expression told me she'd heard the discussion.

She said, "Come here, you handsome hunk," and pulled me toward the couch. She gets crazy every once in a while and calls me something strange like that. We sat down. "Your father doesn't mean to lose his temper like that."

"Then why does he do it?"

"He's under a lot of pressure right now."

"You always say that, always make excuses for him."

"Do I?" She started scratching my back. She knows that's the way to get me to sit still and listen. "I don't know what's going through your dad's mind, but I know it's something he has to resolve himself. He won't talk about it."

"He's so mean. He's so selfish."

"Come on, Brandon, be fair. Who just gave you the money to buy Adidas running shoes for your morning race?"

I wasn't about to give in. "What about Grandpa? It's important to him to go back home. He's going to get too sick to make the trip if we don't go soon and Dad just keeps putting it off."

"I think your father can't face going back down there right now. He's avoided it for too long and now his regret about not having visited more often is keeping him mixed up."

"I don't understand that."

"I'm not sure I do either, but maybe he'll work it out before the quarter break."

She'd stopped scratching, so I wiggled a little to remind her. She started again.

"Why can't we go, just you and Grandpa and me— and leave Dad home?"

"I thought about it, but it wouldn't be right. If we let him get out of it, he'll never go back and face those feelings he's fighting."

"So Grandpa has to suffer?"

She sighed. "In a way, your dad's right. The long trip wouldn't be good for your grandfather. If that whole area down there wasn't so primitive, we could fly. But it's still too far from the nearest decent airport to Grandpa's."

"Are you saying we're stuck here?"

"I guess so . . . at least for a while."

You're wrong, I thought. There's a way to get Grandpa back home and I'm going to find it.

Monday's Memorial Day adventure was as crazy as Ham had promised. Grandfather Berger was loud and embarrassing just as I'd pictured him. At least he took my mind off my troubles at home. At the cemetery, as soon as he set the big arrangement of flowers on the stone, he started talking right out loud to his wife, as though she could hear him from down under the ground.

"I don't know what you were thinking of, Sarah," he said to the grass while Ham and his parents looked around to see who was watching. "How could you think of leaving me alone here on earth for so long, woman? I was a good husband."

Ham said, "I don't think it was her decision to leave, Grandpa."

"Quiet, David. I'm talking to your grandmother," old Mr. Berger said, and then went on. "Was it rest you wanted? I suggested a cleaning lady, but no, you wanted to do everything yourself. Was it my socks? Well, I pick them up now, Sarah, and put them in the hamper myself. So you can just arrange to have me join you, Mrs. Berger. If you're as pushy in heaven as you were down here, you should have no trouble making my reservations."

"Dad," said Ham's father with a blush.

"I'm just being honest, son, telling it like it is as you young people put it. Your mother was a jewel, but she had her faults, rest her soul."

On the way back to the car, old Mr. Berger wandered around, reading headstones. "Just listen to this one," he'd say in a loud voice. Then he'd read the message. "How ridiculous!" he'd say, shaking his head. He didn't care if the people who'd paid for the headstone were standing there or not. No wonder Ham was always afraid of getting punched in the nose when he went out with Grandpa Berger. We all let out a big sigh as the car pulled out of the cemetery.

Although he was loud and embarrassing, I've got to admit, Ham's grandfather was generous.

"Stop at Duerden's Deluxe Ice Cream, son," he said. "These boys need nourishment."

When I ordered a double-scoop cone, he said, "Nonsense, Brandon. Order a banana split, a Super Sundae, a Pig's Delight . . . something with real substance."

As we glanced over the menu once more to find something with substance, Mrs. Berger said, "Grandpa, let the boys choose for themselves."

"Of course," he said in his booming voice. "They can choose anything. Brandon, if you want a cone, go ahead . . . make it two."

"He loves to show off and be the big spender," Ham whispered.

"I like that quality in a grandfather," I said, and we both laughed.

"A private joke?" Mrs. Berger asked, gathering up extra napkins and tucking them in her purse.

"Nothing," Ham said.

We both ordered hot-fudge sundaes.

When they stopped to let me out at home, Ham said, "I'll call you tomorrow. Are you going anywhere?"

"I don't think so," I answered. But as I walked up to the front door I thought, maybe I'll be on my way to Little Water.

# Chapter Ten

On Tuesday morning, my eyes opened automatically before the sun was up. I waited for a minute for Grandpa to call me. There was no sound from the bottom bunk. Finally I rolled over and leaned down to see if he had left me behind this morning. He was still in bed.

"Grandpa?"

Silence.

"*Shinali?*" I said louder, my heart starting its own race.

"Mmm?" He said in answer.

"It's time to run."

He turned slowly and I slid out of bed. Grandpa didn't get up.

"You go, *Shiyazhi.*"

"Are you feeling sick?"

"No. I'm fine." He reached to the floor and picked up the sagebrush twigs. I hadn't noticed them. "I'll meet you when you return," Grandpa said, and brought the sage to his nose.

I felt a strange loneliness, starting out my run without his encouragement. I missed feeling his eyes follow me to the corner, but the rhythm of the running soon brought a sense of harmony. Again I made it farther than before and kept my breathing more even and strong.

Grandfather was waiting on the sidewalk when I turned the corner, and his smile gave me an extra reward for the hard work.

"Today we tend the squash plants," he said, and I followed him over to the flower bed beneath our bedroom window.

The plants were barely pushing through the soil on two mounds and the third didn't even show a crack to indicate that anything was happening beneath the ground.

"I don't know what's wrong with these," I said. "They were planted at almost the same time as the ones in back but they're not even growing."

The squash plants in back were at least three inches high.

"This is the wrong place for them," Grandpa said simply. "They need warmth in the morning that this part of the earth can't give them."

He shook his head slowly. "Plants can't live in a place that's not right for them."

I looked up at his solemn expression. I knew he was thinking that people can't live in a place that's not right for them, either. I was so glad he didn't say it that I didn't even question him when he turned and walked into the house without his usual visit to the backyard. He went straight to our room and lay down on the bunk.

"When are we going to check the other plants?"

"Later," he said with a sigh. "You can check them."

I didn't feel like checking them without him.

"But don't water them," he went on. "I have something to teach you about plants, about the ways of nature. One of those important things. We'll do it later . . . in a little while."

He took a deep breath and closed his eyes. I went to take a shower.

Grandpa didn't get up until ten o'clock. Mom coaxed him until he ate most of the oatmeal that she'd made specially for him. Then we went out to the garden. The bean plants were already pushing upward a couple of inches, and each squash mound had a crown of twisted dark green stems and leaves.

"Watch carefully," Grandpa said as he knelt by the first mound. He sorted through the tangle of small vines, chose one, and pulled it out.

"Hey! What are you doing?" I asked.

He pulled another vine from the tangle and threw it on the grass behind him next to the first one he'd pulled.

"Those are just starting to grow!" I protested. Grandpa just smiled, reached down, and pulled another plant.

"There are two plants left in this hill," he said. "That's good."

"Good? We could've had *five* squash plants there if you hadn't pulled out those other perfectly good ones!"

Grandpa shook his head. "If you leave five plants growing, they'll all be small and weak with few blossoms and skinny squash. The plants must have room to grow so they'll become strong and good, like they're meant to be."

"Then why plant five seeds? You're just wasting squash seeds if you're going to throw three of the plants away."

"You plant five so that you can be sure that squash will grow. Some of the seeds may not be good, they may not send out shoots. With five, you can be certain to have some plants. You can choose the strongest ones to stay and grow big."

"It still seems kind of sad to throw those plants away." I picked up the vines, already wilting in the morning heat.

"It's the way of the earth. Those plants have done good. They have protected their brothers from wind and harsh sun while they were very young. Now that these two are strong, they will grow without the shelter of the ones that are gone."

He stood up and pointed to the next mound. "You choose the strong plants."

I knelt down and took my time finding what looked like the thickest, greenest vines. Grandfather nodded every once in a while.

"You must remember these things, Brandon, because of me."

I looked up at him.

"I'm leaving you soon . . . but you are strong and growing in the right way. You return from your race to the sun each morning with light in your face. You know the good feeling that comes from tired arms and dirt under your fingernails. You'll be all right when I'm gone, but you must remember me so you will keep growing."

I scooted over to the next hill and started sorting through the vines. I couldn't look at my grandfather. "I won't be strong when you're gone," I said at last. "I can't stand to think of you not being here."

He walked up behind me and laid a hand on each of my shoulders. "That's the next important thing you need to know." He laughed. "Your mother told me where you went yesterday, why you paid a visit to the dead ones. I think it's very strange."

"You do?"

"To think of those that lived but live no longer only once a year is not natural. I think of those who gave me life every day, almost all the time now. But even when I was young, I thought of them—the things they did, the things they taught me. And that's how it will be with you."

He patted my shoulders. "My body may be planted in the ground, but I will be here with you. Each time you race the sun or run your hands through dirt or pick a squash plant, I will be here."

A tear plopped on the mound in front of me and quickly disappeared into the dry soil. Then another one fell.

"Don't be sad, *Shiyazhi*. I'm going to another place where I can grow. I'm making room. I am not sad; I'm happy because I've had the chance to become a part of you, to send myself into new life. For a long time I felt that I would never know you, teach you, so I'm glad."

I turned around and hugged his knees. As he pulled me to my feet, I rested my head against his chest and smelled his warm, special scent. I knew I was getting his shirt damp but I didn't want to pull away. I wanted to stand there and feel the comfort of his hands ruffling my hair for a long, long time.

"I'm just a little sad," he said. His voice rumbled in his chest as he talked. "Because I'm here in this strange place. I love you and your mother and your father, my son. But I belong at home."

I pulled away and looked up to see his eyes wet again.

"I know you do," I said. "We're going there. I'm going to take you home."

He smiled and shook his head. "Only in my thoughts, I'm afraid."

"I have a plan," I said, and all of a sudden, I *did* have a plan. It was crazy but it would work. It had to work!

"Have you lost your mind?" Ham asked me later that afternoon. "Nobody kidnaps his own grandfather."

"Desperate problems call for desperate solutions." I read that in a book once.

"I won't deny that you have a big problem," he said. I'd told him everything, starting with Kee Redhouse becoming Keith Rogers and finishing with my grandfather being sick and talking about dying. He'd sat there for all that time and listened without a yawn. He'd even handed me his clean handkerchief when I started getting teary like some dopey little kid and he didn't say one teasing word. That's what a best friend is like.

"Besides, I'm not really kidnapping him. I mean, I'm really sort of helping him run away."

"Are you sure it's going to do any good, running away to the reservation with your grandpa?" Ham held a bag of cookies out to me, but I shook my head. "Even if you get your grandfather to Little Water on the bus, your dad's just going to come right down there and get you guys and bring you back."

"That's OK. Even if Dad gets all mad about it, Grandpa will still get to see the reservation one more time, spend a little while down there. That's all he really wants. I don't think he'll mind being dragged back to the city if he gets a chance to fix Little Water in his mind again."

"If he's as sick as you say, can he take that bus trip?"

"He'll manage," I said. "He's tougher than he looks. Besides, there's something giving him strength; it's not physical. It seems more . . . spiritual. I don't know how to explain it."

"Don't try. I trust your intuition." He stood up. "I've got to go, but I want to help. If you need it, I've got a little money stashed away at home. . . ."

I shook my head. "No, but thanks anyway. I'm going to the bank now and get some out of my college account."

"Can you do that? My mother has to sign for me to get any of my savings out."

"Thank goodness my folks are sold on this modern independence stuff. My dad keeps pushing me to do things on my own. It was his idea to make me totally responsible for the account. He wants to show how much he trusts me."

"And what does his trustworthy son do behind his back?" Ham asked on his way out of the family room. "Steal his father!"

Grandpa was sitting on the patio, singing softly to himself.

"Do you want to go for a walk, *Shinali?*"

"Where?"

"Over to the mall."

He looked hesitant, probably remembering the last

99

time he'd been over there and some jerk had ignored him.

"I'm going to the bank to get some money. On the way I'll tell you how we're going to get you home to Little Water."

A smile lit his face, and he stood up.

"Are you sure you feel like going?"

"I've felt like going for many days," he said. I was talking about going to the bank and Grandpa was talking about going to Little Water, but since he showed more energy than he had for quite a while, we headed for the mall.

The teller at the bank didn't even question my withdrawal slip for two hundred dollars. I guess he was used to modern, independent kids. He looked over my shoulder at Grandpa sitting by the door.

"That's my grandfather," I said.

He just smiled and nodded.

"He's a Navajo," I added, just so there wouldn't be any question. "Me, too."

The teller smiled politely, but I could tell he was puzzled by my explanation. The whole thing was clear to me. I was making sure that I'd never be ashamed of myself or where I came from again. Not for Grandpa's peace of mind, for mine.

"Notice the earrings? Genuine turquoise," I said.

The guy continued to smile uneasily.

"I might get a pair myself," I said, grinning.

Finally the teller gave me an honest smile. "Why not?" he said.

When we got outside I said, "I think everything is arranged, except a way to get to the bus station. It's too far to walk and too complicated to ride the city bus. It's too risky to call a taxi.''

"I can walk," Grandpa said.

"Don't worry, *Shinali*. I'll think of something."

# Chapter Eleven

Mrs. Berger solved our transportation problem. She was scheduled to meet with one of her many women's clubs and was happy to have us along for company.

"But remember, you're putting your life on the line, riding with my mother," Ham said. "She has trouble talking and driving at the same time and you ought to know by now she won't give up the talking."

I laughed at his exaggeration.

"Laugh while you still can, old friend," he said, patting my shoulder. "Next time we meet, you might be lying in a hospital bed with your jaw wired shut."

A few hours later, Mrs. Berger's white Continental lurched to a stop in front of our house, and I looked at Grandpa. He didn't seem worried, but of course he hadn't had much experience with city traffic.

"Oh, I'm so glad you two are going my way," Ham's mother began before we were even settled in the car, Grandpa in the back and me up front. "I tell David

**103**

he should come with me. He could go to a movie or visit the museum, find something to occupy his time while I'm in my meeting." She looked over and smiled. "But he just tells me he has things to do and can't waste all that time just to be my audience on the drive downtown. Audience, he says. I'm not quite sure what he means by that."

She switched lanes, and I heard a screech behind us. "Oh, dear," she said, looking in her rearview mirror. Then, "Believe me, I'm just very happy to have somebody along to visit with. It gives me a chance to warm up my voice for the discussion I have to lead." She looked over again. "Do you two have any ideas for renovating Springbrook Park?" The car drifted over the center line, and an oncoming car's horn drew her attention back to the road.

"Whoops! So, where are you going? It doesn't look like you've packed for a two-week cruise." She laughed again.

I'd put one change of clothes for each of us into my backpack, thinking we'd attract less attention sneaking away without real luggage. My folks could bring along more clothes after we called them and told them where we were. For sure, they'd be coming down to bring us back.

"No, ma'am," I said. "We're just meeting my father downtown. He's taking us to dinner and then to a lecture." I gestured toward the pack. "This is just some books and papers he wanted."

"Isn't that nice?" Mrs. Berger said, noticing a stop sign at the last minute and slamming on her brakes. I put my hand on the dashboard and held myself back against the seat just in case the seat belt didn't hold.

After two more stop signs, I decided to leave my hand there for support, physical and emotional.

Actually, my dad and mom were at a faculty dinner for a professor who was retiring. I was hoping they'd get home late and just peek in to see that Grandpa and I were all right. We'd left blankets rolled under our covers just like runaways in the movies. If they were tired enough, my parents wouldn't bother to check the lumps too closely.

"So, how do you like the big city, Mr. Rogers?" Ham's mother asked my grandfather, turning to peer into the backseat.

"Fine. Lots of nice houses here," he said.

My alarmed gasp prompted Mrs. Berger to face forward just in time to swerve around a guy on a motorcycle. A tinny beep of his horn registered his futile protest.

The whole ride was like that, nonstop conversation punctuated by near-misses with cars, bicycles, pedestrians, and shrubbery. I was so relieved when we made it to the destination I'd arranged with Ham's mother, two blocks from the bus station, that I almost cartwheeled out of the car.

"Thanks very much, Mrs. Berger," I said through the window with my feet planted safely on the curb.

"My pleasure. Are you sure you don't want a ride home? If your father gets delayed or can't make it or something, I'll be happy to give you a lift. I can write down the number of where I'll be, if you want."

"That's OK. My dad's very dependable. He'll be here."

"Have a good time," she called as she pulled into traffic, cutting in front of a delivery truck. I could have sworn she was talking to herself, but maybe she was

**105**

saying something to the driver of the truck because his horn was so loud.

We had plenty of time before our bus left, so we walked to the station at a leisurely pace. I had Grandpa sit down on a bench while I bought the bus tickets. Then I joined him. He looked tired, but every few minutes a peaceful smile would light up his face. Our boarding call finally rasped over the static-plagued speaker, and we climbed aboard. I was relieved that the bus wasn't crowded. We sat toward the back, and I let *Shinali* sit next to the window so he wouldn't be bothered by aisle traffic.

We didn't talk. I watched the few passengers choose their seats while Grandpa looked out the window.

The door shut and the driver raced the engine. Then he took his foot from the gas pedal and opened the door again. A huge sunburned man carrying a couple of blankets and a pillow climbed aboard. He puffed his way down the aisle, and when he saw Grandpa and me, his face lit up in a smile. I looked at the floor. Because of my dad's job, I'm always being recognized by people I don't remember meeting. As the bus pulled out, the man lunged into the seat across the aisle from me. From the corner of my eye all I could see was a huge stomach hanging over a wide belt and faded jeans.

"Navajo, aren't you?" he said, setting his bedding on the seat next to the window and leaning forward so he could see us better.

I nodded.

"I thought so. I can always spot a Navajo. They're fine people."

I didn't respond. If I acted too friendly, I might have to talk to him all the way to Little Water.

"I was raised among them, you know," the man went on. "My father ran a trading post. Hell, I didn't know what a White man was till I went to school in town."

He rubbed his thighs as though trying to restore his circulation. Maybe his belt was too tight.

"Yes, sir, my dad treated those Navajos around there just like they were members of the family. Always had an extra place set at the table just in case one of them needed a square meal."

"Hmm," I said.

"Look at this," the man said, holding his stomach out of the way so I could see a silver belt buckle with turquoise stones. "My Navajo brother made it for me. By dang, we were closer than real brothers."

He leaned farther forward to look at my grandfather. *"Ya´at´eeh, Shichei,"* he said loudly. *"Haadee nanina?* Where are you from?" Then he turned to me. "Does the old man speak English?"

I nodded.

"Must be hard of hearing."

"He isn't feeling very well," I explained.

"Oh, I get it," the man said.

I wasn't sure what he meant by that, but at least he leaned back and stopped talking.

Grandpa sat up and turned to him. *"Ya´at´eeh, sik´is."* He extended his hand, and the man shook it. When *Shinali* sank back into the seat, I noticed the man wiping his hands on his jeans. Maybe it was a nervous gesture.

The man remained quiet until we'd left the city behind.

"Better let him sleep," he told me.

I nodded.

An hour later we stopped at a small town, and a

woman and her little girl got on. They took the seat in front of the fat man.

He talked to them for a few minutes, asking where they were going and praising the fun of making new friends on a bus trip. I wondered if the woman were starting to regret her seat selection. The man gestured toward Grandfather and me. "These two are Indians, you know. Navajos."

The woman gave us an embarrassed smile.

"Hell, I was raised among those people. Even had a Navajo brother."

Like me, the woman didn't know how to respond to his comments, so she didn't say anything.

"They're a hard people to get close to, I'll tell you. But once you win their trust, they're your friends till they die. My daddy spent his life working with them, trying to help them better themselves. A lot of people think they're lazy but I've seen young bucks that would work all day in the hot sun just for a sack of flour."

The woman finally spoke. "A sack of flour? Is that what your father paid a man for his day's work?"

The man chuckled. "I can see you don't understand Indians at all, ma'am. Sometimes Daddy'd have to take care of them just like little children. He'd give them credit at the trading post for the work they'd done, but if he gave them money, they'd hightail it to town and get drunk."

The man leaned forward so his face was close to the woman. "That's what's wrong with that old guy," he said softly.

The woman looked at us more closely.

"My grandfather is sick," I said, not caring if they

**108**

believed me or not, hating them for talking about us as though we couldn't hear or understand.

The man sat back. "He's sick, all right," he said, lifting his fist with the thumb extended toward his mouth and making a glugging sound.

In a minute the woman leaned toward me. "I think your grandfather would be more comfortable with a pillow. Why don't you fix this one so he can rest against the window and get some sleep." She glanced at the man behind her, then said to me, "If I had a blanket, I'd let him use it, but I don't."

The man didn't respond.

"That's OK," I said. "Thanks for the pillow."

"Is there anything else I can do?"

"No, but thanks. The pillow will help a lot."

"Should he be traveling? He looks so tired, kind of feverish."

"I know," I said. "But he has to get home. He'll feel better when he gets there."

She didn't say any more, just gave me a sympathetic smile and turned to face forward.

*Shinali* slept for an hour, and when his eyes opened, I ask him how he was doing.

"Fine."

"I hope that stupid guy didn't make you feel bad."

Grandpa smiled. "Don't worry. I've known many stupid men." He pulled my head toward him so he could whisper to me. "Don't be mad at him, *Sitsuie*. He doesn't know any better. He lived among the Navajo but he never knew us. He saw us through his father's eyes, the eyes of his grandfather, and everyone who came before him. Maybe the woman's kindness will change his eyes, he'll see more clearly."

**109**

I doubt it, I thought, but I didn't say it.

Grandpa leaned back and was quiet for so long that I thought he'd gone back to sleep. Then he said, "When I close my eyes and feel the movement of the bus, I remember going away to school when I was young. I can see the land slipping away behind me and new land, strange new sights coming to me as I travel."

"Was it awful, going away to school, leaving your family?"

"Not awful. A little sad, but I liked school. I learned lots of new things, made many friends, not just Navajos but people from many tribes, a few Whites, too."

He shifted in the seat, trying to get comfortable.

"I was always glad to get home. The closer we came to the reservation, the more happy I would feel. I have that same feeling now."

I smiled.

"When your father went to school, I thought it would be like that for him. He'd learn new things but still be happy to come back home. I don't know what happened, but something made him forget the important things."

"He still speaks Navajo, Grandpa."

"I know. He speaks it slowly with a lot of thought, a lot of twisting with his mind and tongue." He sighed. "His Navajo isn't smooth, but that's not one of the important things he forgot."

"Then what?"

"He forgot to like himself. He forgot to smile when he looked back at what he'd been. He tried to be someone completely new instead of building on what he was. And now he's not happy."

Grandpa rubbed his face before going on. "I don't

**110**

know why he thinks I want him to speak Navajo and live in a hogan. I don't. I just want him to be himself, a mixture of Navajo and the new things he's learned. I don't want him to be ashamed that he was once Kee Redhouse, the boy who ran to greet the sun and came back glowing from that race.''

I reached over and patted his thin hand. ''Maybe we can help him see that the whole man, Kee-Keith-Redhouse-Rogers, is a pretty terrific person.''

Grandpa smiled. ''Your father thinks that I disapprove of a house with three bathrooms. That's not so. I think that three bathrooms is more than one family needs, but I don't disapprove. I just wish your father didn't look down on me because I have only one outhouse.''

''One outhouse!'' I said, trying to cheer him up. ''How are we going to survive the next few days?!''

He laughed.

The bus stopped at a restaurant about ten o'clock, but Grandpa didn't feel like getting off. I thought I'd wait with him for a little while before going in to get him something to eat. While we were sitting there, the man from across the aisle climbed back on with a cup of soup.

''I . . . I brought some hot soup for your grandfather,'' he said.

''No, thanks.'' I looked out the window.

''It's not bad . . . for restaurant soup. You might even find a piece of chicken in there.''

I continued to stare out into the dark. Grandpa leaned over and nudged me with his elbow.

''I think it will give him some strength,'' the man said softly.

"*Ahe´he*. Thank you," Grandpa said, sitting up.

"About before . . ." The man slipped his hands into his back pockets and rocked on his heels. "I apologize. Sometimes I talk too damned much . . . but I don't really mean it. The buffalo chips just roll right out of my mouth before I think."

I laughed and he joined in.

"*Ahe´he, sik´is*. Thank you very much," my grandfather said again, and the man went back to the cafe.

After *Shinali* finished, we went in to the rest room. On the way out, I ordered a hamburger and ate it after the bus started up again. The man across the aisle insisted that I cover Grandpa with one of his blankets, and in a few minutes *Shinali* started to doze, talking Navajo softly to himself. I leaned my seat back and let the motion of the bus and Grandpa's voice help me relax. Soon I was asleep.

I guess when the man and the woman and little girl left the bus, they didn't want to disturb my grandfather. I woke up a few hours later and checked on him. The blanket and pillow were still there, but the owners were gone.

# Chapter Twelve

The bus rolled into town at four o'clock the next morning. There were people meeting a few of the scruffy, bleary-eyed passengers, but of course we had no one waiting for us. We eased ourselves down the steps, into the cold fresh air, and went inside.

The place could hardly be called a bus station. It was a small adobe building with bars on its two tiny windows. The interior was a single room painted dull brown. There was a counter in front of a storage room, and the door next to the counter said "Restroo-."

"Now what?" I asked Grandpa. Little Water is actually twenty miles from the town where the bus stops, and believe me, there's no taxicab service.

"In the morning, we'll hitch a ride," he said confidently. "Until then we sit here and wait."

"Are you sure we'll be able to catch a ride?"

He smiled. "We're home, *Sitsuie*. We have lots of relatives who'll be going our way."

113

I set the pillow down on one of the wooden benches that lined the walls to make a soft seat for Grandpa and draped the blanket over his shoulders.

The man from the ticket counter locked all the doors, checked the rest room, and finally approached us.

"You'll have to leave. This place is only open at night for a few minutes each time a bus comes in." He wiped his red eyes and laughed. "Three times in all." He continued, more to himself than to us, "What a schedule! In here for forty-five minutes, home for an hour, back here for the L.A. bus, then . . ." He noticed we were still listening. "Sorry, I know it's not your problem. I wish I'd get that transfer to Phoenix."

He looked at his watch, then back at us.

I sighed and glanced at my grandfather.

"It's nothing personal, but I can't have a bunch of people sitting around in here with no one to keep an eye on things." He was studying Grandpa.

I stood up and turned to help *Shinali*.

"Look. Do you have somebody coming to pick you up?"

"I think so," I said.

"All right, you can stick around for a few minutes. It's not that cold outside, but there's no decent place to sit down." He looked at the clock above a tattered poster showing the somewhat faded splendor of the Grand Canyon. "I'm not about to hang around on my own time, but if you make sure that the door locks when you leave, I guess it will be all right. Don't let anyone else in, OK?"

"Sure."

"I'm going to turn out the main lights and leave the night-lights on. Is that all right?"

**114**

"That's fine," I said with relief. "And thanks, thanks a lot."

He just shrugged and hurried to douse the bright lights. Then he left.

We sat in the dark, empty room, leaning against one another, hardly talking but feeling comfortable in the silence. Who would have thought that in three weeks I could become so close to my strange old Navajo grandfather? Sometimes I felt that I knew what he was thinking so he didn't have to say it, not specific things, but the general direction of his thoughts. Maybe a lot of those thoughts were becoming my own. I didn't think I'd ever make the reservation my home. I wasn't about to give up indoor plumbing for an outhouse, but I had to admit I liked the smell of sage and cedar smoke.

At six I placed a collect call to my parents. My father answered the phone.

"Where are you?" he asked, ignoring the operator.

"Will you pay for the call?" she said again.

"Yes, yes, of course."

"Go ahead," she said.

"Dad, look, I'm sorry to wake you up but . . ."

"Where are you?" The grogginess was leaving his voice. "At eleven last night you were sound asleep in bed."

"Actually, at eleven we were on a bus . . ."

"A what?"

"We were on a bus, on our way to Little Water. That's where we are right now. Well, not Little Water, in town . . . at the bus station."

"If this is some kind of joke, Brandon, I'm going to kill you."

I could hear my mother's voice in the background asking questions.

"No joke, Dad. Grandpa just had to get home . . . so I decided to bring him down here."

"You took your grandfather on a bus all the way to the reservation?! What in the world were you thinking? He could have died!"

There was a pause while he relayed the information to my mother.

"How is he?"

I looked over at my grinning grandfather. "He's OK, Dad. Honest, he looks better than he has for a week."

My mother came on the line. "Brandon? We're coming down."

There was a brief argument that I couldn't hear very well because my mother had her hand over the receiver. "Your dad and I will make some arrangements for his classes and throw some things in a suitcase and be on our way." She placed her hand over the receiver again for a minute. "Have you got a way to get out to Grandpa's?"

"Don't worry. We'll find a way. We have lots of relatives down here." I smiled at *Shinali*. "Mom? Bring me some clothes, anything. We didn't have time to pack."

"Do you want her to bring your boxes?" I asked my grandfather.

"I won't need them."

"We'll be down late today, probably evening," Mom said. "Be careful. . . ."

My father started talking to her again, but I couldn't make out what he was saying.

**116**

"Your dad wants to say something," she said. "Take care of yourself, Brandon . . . and take care of Grandpa."

"I will."

I could hear Dad breathing into the phone for about thirty seconds before he spoke. "Be careful, Brandon."

"We will."

"And, son . . ." I waited for a few moments. "Tell Grandpa that I love him."

"I will, Dad. We'll see you tonight."

I don't know if it was mental telepathy or what, but we walked right out to the highway, I stuck out my thumb for a ride, and the very first pickup truck stopped for us. My grandfather talked to the people in the cab for a few minutes in Navajo, then he turned to me.

"This is my nephew's in-laws. They're going out home. I told you we'd find a ride."

I helped him climb into the back, then jumped in myself. The driver waited while we got settled on a stack of blankets next to the cab, out of the wind, and we started out.

In a minute my grandfather pointed to the sky. "I'm home, *Sitsuie*." A hawk circled through the clear air far above us. "Soon your father will be home, too. I know he's only coming for a visit, but it's a very important visit. He'll have time to get to know this place again."

"He's not going to stay for very long, Grandpa."

"He will stay. He'll stay to say good-bye to me, to put me in the ground."

Although they were already tied, I started fixing my shoelaces, trying to get them exactly even.

"Don't talk like that, *Shinali*. You're going to be all right."

**117**

He smiled. "I'll be all right, but I'm leaving this place."

"Are you scared?"

"A little. Like going to school, scared but excited about the new places I will see, new things I'll learn."

I finished with my shoes.

"You never told me about death, about the Happy Hunting Ground and all that stuff."

Grandpa looked at my solemn face and laughed. "You've seen too many movies. The only happy hunting ground I know is over by Flagstaff where the deer are fat and not too quick."

I laughed.

"I'm not sure about death, Brandon. I know lots of things that people say about it but I think I'll have to find out what it's like myself."

He sighed. "I'll miss you . . . all my family. But I'm anxious to get started."

I gave him a worried glance.

"Not right now, *Sitsuie*. Don't worry." He grinned. "Now, let's talk of important things again. You must make your father know how proud I am of him. I'm pleased with Keith Rogers, his fine job, and his three bathrooms," he said, and laughed. "Tell him that I'm also proud of Kee Redhouse, who used to herd sheep and chop wood and listen to the old stories."

"If you'll just wait around for a few hours, you can tell him yourself, Grandpa. He'll listen this time, I know he will." A tight feeling of panic kept pounding its way into my chest.

"Somehow make him understand that I love him, I always loved him," Grandpa said, and then he settled

**118**

back and watched the reservation slip past the sides of the pickup.

When we turned from the highway onto the dirt road, Grandpa sat up. The truck had to go slower because of ruts and bumps. My grandfather concentrated on each bush, every tree and rock. It was as though he were memorizing every inch of the way back to his home.

Stopping the pickup, the driver rolled down his window and shouted to us in Navajo. My grandfather answered him, and we drove on.

"He wanted to know if I was going home or to Ethel's house."

"What did you tell him?"

"Ethel's house."

In a few minutes the pickup was escorted up the family road by three barking dogs. As we pulled up in front of the house, a young face appeared at a window. Then the whole family flooded out the door to welcome Grandpa. I recognized Aunt Ethel and Uncle Stanley, of course, and Alex because he's my age. I couldn't remember the names of the two boys and three girls whose excited smiles kept getting interrupted by happy bursts of chatter in Navajo.

The pickup drove back down, leaving the whole group standing in its dust, hugging, shaking hands, talking. Aunt Ethel's was just an ordinary frame house, except for its bright blue color. The front door was in the middle of the house, and a wooden porch ran to one end. In front of the house toward the other end, the front and back seats from a junked car leaned against the wall. While the others were catching up on current events in Navajo, I went over, sat down, and started

**119**

scratching a brown and white mongrel dog behind the ears.

I felt nervous and out of place. My aunt and uncle have always been nice to me, but we've never stayed long enough for me to get very well acquainted with them or my cousins. My one memory of playing there is when Alex let me ride his bike without telling me the brakes didn't work. I wasn't used to reservation roads anyway, and in my panic at not being able to slow down, I crashed into a boulder, finally bouncing into a nearby sagebrush. Alex and the other kids laughed like crazy and talked in Navajo, retelling my mishap again and again. I knew they were talking about it because of their gestures and sound effects. That was one time I didn't mind it when Dad called, "Let's go."

I wasn't holding that incident against my cousins. I'd have laughed at the accident myself, if I were them, but I still felt lost. What was I going to do all day while Grandpa visited and I waited for my parents to show up?

In a little while Grandpa came over. The others went into the house. The dog moved over to sniff at my grandfather's knees. He stood there for a few moments, wagging his long shaggy tail, then wandered off.

"The children will be leaving pretty soon; schools aren't out for the summer yet. Stan and Ethel have to go to work, too. It will be quiet here then."

"You mean they aren't going to stick around today, take a day off so they can visit with you?"

"It's better this way," he said. "We've visited all our lives."

Aunt Ethel came out, pushing beaded combs in her hair to hold it back from her face. "I think I can take the day off, Dad, if you want me to."

**120**

"No, you go to work. We'll be fine."

"There's food in the house. The kids will be home at four and I'll be here soon after that."

"*Hagoshii*," Grandpa said.

The children, including Alex, hurried out. After a flurry of good-byes, they started down the road to catch the school bus. Uncle Stanley got into the pickup and left for work, and Ethel went back in to finish getting ready.

"When Ethel leaves, we'll go over to my house."

"Are you sure you don't want to rest first?"

"I'm sure." He got up and went into the house. In a minute he returned with an old canvas bag with FIRST NATIONAL BANK and a logo stamped on it. "My jewelry. Ethel's been keeping it for me."

He untied the drawstring and felt around inside, finally pulling out a silver bracelet with three turquoise stones.

"I made this a long time ago," he said.

"I didn't know you were a silversmith!"

"There's still a lot about me you don't know, but you will find out. Your father will tell you."

My expression was skeptical.

"You ask him," *Shinali* said. "He'll tell you."

He dug in the bag again and brought out a second bracelet, identical to the first. "There are only two. They are my design, my creation."

He handed one to me.

"It's beautiful," I said, admiring the intricate details— leaves, ropes, swirls of silver surrounding the oval stones. I held it out to him.

"No, it's yours . . . so you will not forget me."

"I don't need this to remind me of you, Grandpa."

**121**

"I know that." He grinned. "You know the important things we talked about already. But this bracelet is meant to be yours. I've been keeping it for you."

"I don't know what to say . . . thanks." I put it on my wrist. It was loose, but I'd grow into it.

Grandpa put the other bracelet on his wrist just as Aunt Ethel came out.

"You two take care of each other," she said.

We stood up and Ethel hugged Grandpa tightly for a few seconds. "I love you, *Shizhe´e.*"

"Yes," he said. *"Shi doo´."*

Then she gave me a hug, too. Mothers are all alike; they have an uncontrollable urge to wrap their arms around someone. She got in her dusty car and drove off.

# Chapter Thirteen

Grandfather and I stood in front of the bright blue house and watched the dust settle into the ruts of the country road that served as a driveway for my aunt and uncle. Grandpa sighed, and I looked over into his tired face.

"Let's go home," he said, releasing another sigh and rubbing his eyes with both hands.

"I think we ought to rest for a little while," I said. "We have lots of time."

He looked at the sun inching above the mesa top.

"Come on, *Shinali*. Just a short nap and we'll start for your house before the day gets too warm. I'll feel a lot better after some rest."

Grandpa chuckled. "We'll rest, then." He started toward the house. "I know that you feel fine, *Sitsuie* . . . except for your worry about me." He turned back to me. "You're right, there is time. It's better to rest for a while."

He went into the one big room that served as a bedroom for all the kids. Two sets of bunk beds and one double bed were pushed against the walls along with two mismatched chests of drawers. For sure, privacy wasn't very easy to come by in the Benally household. Each cousin had tried to individualize his area of the room by decorating the space around his bed. I guessed that one set of bunk beds belonged to Alex and his brother because of the National Indian Rodeo Association posters and pictures of motorcycles on the wall next to it.

Grandpa lay down on the girls' double bed with a hundred pictures cut from teenage magazines looking down on him. He was asleep almost immediately.

Standing in the middle of the room, I tried to get used to the quiet. There was no traffic noise, no lawn mower chugging or door slamming, no sound of music drifting from a neighbor's house. I wasn't sure where the nearest neighbor was. I'd always thought of my own house and neighborhood as quiet, but this place was almost eerie in its silence. I listened to the slow breathing of my grandfather for a few minutes. Then there was a click and the refrigerator rattled to life in the other room. I decided to get acquainted with the house.

It didn't take long because there were only two more rooms. One was a small bedroom for Uncle Stanley and Aunt Ethel. I felt snoopy as I peeked in the door at the unmade bed, the chest of drawers with clothes spilling from it, and the nightstand where photographs of family members fought for breathing room among bottles of lotion and cologne. I went into the other room, a combination kitchen and living room that took up half the house. The white door of the small refrigerator was covered with children's artwork, crayon flowers with "I love you, Mother" across the top of the paper, a stick-figure boy herding lumpy sheep with twiglike legs. Cupboards with counter space beneath them stood along the wall next to the fridge, and across the room a white stove shared space with the rickety wooden box that served as a stand for a rectangular stainless-steel sink.

I walked around a formica dining set to get a drink. Although the sink had a drain, there was no faucet. Looking at the big blue cooking pan with a cup turned upside down on its lid, I remembered that my aunt and uncle had to haul their water in big metal drums. As I dipped myself a drink of still-cool water from the pan and replaced the lid, I examined the rest of the room. At the opposite end, there was a worn sofa with a coffee table in front of it. The top of the table was piled with magazines and newspapers. There were two chairs, a sagging old-timer that matched the sofa and a brand new recliner covered in red vinyl. More pictures of family members covered one wall, and under the windows on the opposite wall stood a television set. A large tapestry of the Last Supper hung behind the couch.

I set the cup back on the water pan, listened at the door of the big bedroom to Grandpa's exhausted breathing, then went outside.

The brown and white dog sidled up to me. His energetic tail seemed to wag the whole back end of his body.

"What's your name?" I asked just to hear some sound.

He pushed his head between my hand and leg in a

**125**

pathetic attempt to get affection. I scratched him on the neck and behind the ears.

"I think I'll call you Tailwind," I said, watching his tail spin.

He didn't care what I called him as long as I kept scratching.

I picked up a stick. "Do you know any tricks?" Holding the stick over my head, I said, "Get ready, boy. We're going to play fetch."

I threw the stick. "Go get it, Tailwind. Get the stick."

He turned and watched the stick bounce along the sand, then turned back to me.

"You're not much of a dog," I said. He pushed his nose against my hand. "No more petting. I don't want you getting used to all this attention. I'm not going to be around here very long."

He followed me to the outhouse at the far side of the woodpile. When I came out, he was still waiting.

He walked right beside me all the way back to the house and whined when I went inside.

Sitting on the dilapidated sofa in the living room, I decided that TV might disturb Shinali, so I read through a stack of *Western Horseman*. After learning all I'd ever want to know about hoof diseases, bridle and bit combinations, and rodeo events, I lay down to rest my eyes. The hum of the refrigerator lulled me to sleep.

Grandpa and I must have been more tired than I thought. The sound of talking was the next thing I heard. When I sat up, the magazine I'd been reading earlier came with me, stuck to my arm with perspiration. Walking over to the window, I wiped more sweat from my forehead, then my upper lip. The kids came up the road in a noisy group. Alex held onto the backpack of one of his little brothers so the kid couldn't go forward. When the boy screamed, Alex let go. The kid stumbled forward a few steps and Alex laughed. When my little cousin started walking, Alex grabbed onto the pack again.

I went to check on *Shinali*. The bedroom was even hotter than the other room. Grandpa lay on his back on a damp pillow. His face was shiny with sweat, and little drops of it slid into the creases in his face. I checked one of the windows to see how it opened. It had a nail hammered in the frame to keep it shut. Navajo security system, I thought.

When the kids burst through the front door, Grandpa stirred, then rubbed his hands over his wet face.

*"Ayoo deestoi,"* he said. "It's like a sweat bath."

"I'm sorry, *Shinali*. I guess we overslept."

"That's OK. I feel good. We'll go to my house in a little while, when the sun is not so high."

"I know you were in a hurry." I looked at the other window. It had a nail lock, too. "Now the kids are home and Ethel and Stan will be here pretty soon. Maybe my dad and mom will get here, too. I hope they don't give you a big hassle about wanting to go home."

Grandpa smiled. "That's what life is all about— problems. Hassles, you call them. The trick is to keep working through the problems, never giving up." He sat up slowly. "There's a pattern to living, *Sitsuie*. Things work out the way they're supposed to. A change of plans in going to my home is just a surprise in the pattern. Everything will work out right."

The kids were clinking glasses, opening the refrigerator, slamming cupboards. Alex looked surprised when he walked through the door with a stack of cookies in one hand and a glass of milk in the other.

"Hi," I said.

He tipped his head back to get the cookie that was hanging on his lip into his mouth. "Hi. Did we wake you guys up? I'm sorry about being so noisy. I forgot you were here."

"That's OK. We've been sleeping all day."

He spoke to Grandpa in Navajo.

After *Shinali* answered in Navajo, he said, "Yes, I feel better. It was a good sleep. It's good to hear wind in cedar and piñon trees, to smell sagebrush."

I hadn't heard any noise at all until the kids got home, and the only odors I could detect were a kind of sweaty smell and the chocolate from Alex's Oreos. I guess city life dampens your senses.

"Do you want some cookies and milk?"

"Just milk," Grandpa said.

"Cecelia," Alex called into the other room, "get Grandpa a glass of milk." He looked over at me.

"Nothing for me, thanks." I was hungry but still felt shy around this new place. "I was going to open a window, but they're nailed shut."

Alex set his glass on the dresser and stacked the cookies next to it. He gave me a smile, walked to the window, easily pulled the nail out of the frame, and slid the window open.

I didn't know if the smile was friendly or a superior smirk, but I gave him the benefit of the doubt and smiled back.

"Do you want to try the other window on your own, city boy, or should I do it?"

I stopped smiling and opened the other window.

**128**

"Nice bracelet," Alex said, pointing at my outstretched arm with the cookie he'd picked up.

"Thanks." I glanced at Grandpa. He had lain back on the bed and closed his eyes. "I haven't had it very long."

"I'll bet." My cousin had another mocking grin on his face. "I'm surprised that you could pry the White man's Seiko off your wrist to make room for a Navajo bracelet."

I held out my other arm with my watch on it. "Surprise! It's a Timex!"

Alex didn't smile. The joke didn't relax him the way I'd hoped it would. He just looked at me and quietly chewed his Oreo.

For the next few minutes I pretended to be fascinated by the view from the window. What a relief it was when Aunt Ethel arrived and Alex went into the other room to meet her.

For the next hour, while everyone stayed busy fixing dinner, I sat on the foot of Grandpa's bed and listened to him hum and chant softly to himself.

Then my folks arrived, and the Benally Welcome Wagon poured outside to do their thing. The greeting was a little less exuberant than the one for *Shinali* but just as warm. Grandpa stayed in the bedroom and my parents went in for a little while to check on him. When they came back out front, my mom said she wanted to hear all about the bus trip, but I was just getting warmed up, only halfway through the ride with Mrs. Berger, when we got interrupted.

"I'll tell you all about it later," I said.

Aunt Ethel gave what sounded like an order in Navajo, and everyone headed for the house.

**129**

"Dinner's ready," Dad said, putting his arm across my shoulders and walking me toward the house.

Uncle Stanley was directing everyone to a seat. "Go tell Grandpa that dinner's ready, Alex," he said.

I started toward the other room, but Alex's expression made it clear that he didn't need any help.

"Grandpa said he isn't hungry. We're supposed to go ahead and eat," Alex reported as we were passing around plates of broiled mutton and fried potatoes. "He just wants to rest for a little longer."

Everybody exchanged concerned looks, but no one said anything. After a few minutes conversation got started again.

There was watermelon for dessert, and we took thick slices out to the front porch. The sun was behind the house and it was cool in the shade.

"I think I'll go take Dad a plate," my father said, wiping his mouth, then his hands, on a paper towel. "Want to give me a hand, son?"

I followed him into the house, and he spooned a few potatoes onto a plate next to a small slice of melon while I poured a half glass of milk. Then we went into the bedroom.

*Shinali* sat up as we came in.

"We brought you some dinner," my dad said.

*"Ahe´he, Shiye´.* I would have come out to eat but I'm not too hungry right now."

"You've got to keep your strength up, Dad." He handed the plate to *Shinali*.

Grandpa took a piece of potato and chewed it slowly.

"I've been resting all day . . . keeping my strength up. It's time to go over to my house."

"Come on, Dad. You're here at Ethel's. Isn't that

**130**

enough to satisfy you? We've been worried sick about you all day, about the strain this crazy whim of coming home has placed on your body.''

Grandpa smiled. ''My body is much better, now that it is home on the reservation.'' He took a bite of watermelon. After swallowing, he went on. ''I'm glad that you've come home, too, Kee . . . Keith. You'll be happy that you made this visit. Just a few days can make a big difference in the pattern of somebody's whole lifetime.''

My dad released an exasperated sigh. ''We don't have a *few days* to waste around here. You're coming back with Helen and me tomorrow . . . back to where the doctors can keep an eye on you, make you comfortable.''

*Shinali* smiled again. ''I'm already comfortable.'' He ate another bite of melon. ''Of course, I'll be more comfortable in a little while . . . when I'm in my own home.''

''You are so stubborn, *Shizhe´e.*'' My dad started talking Navajo, and Grandpa answered him. They talked for a few minutes, at times sounding angry and at others laughing softly.

Finally Dad said, ''All right. You win this battle. We'll take you over to your place for the night, but tomorrow we head back to our home. Agreed?''

Grandpa just smiled.

The day's rest must have done him good. He stood right up and headed out the door with Dad and me following.

The others were surprised to see him. Ethel stood up and offered him the old wooden chair she'd been sitting in.

**131**

"We've got to go," Grandpa said, declining her offer. "I need to get home before dark."

"We'll take you over in the car, Dad," my father said.

Grandpa shook his head. "No, it's a good time to walk, to see things clearly . . . close up." He turned to me. "Brandon will go with me. He'll help me if I get tired."

Alex jumped up. "I'll come too, Grandpa. You might need both of us."

Again *Shinali* shook his head. "Just Brandon tonight, *Sitsuie*." He went over and put his hands on Alex's shoulders the way he had done to me so often. "We've had a lifetime together, Alex. This night must be for Brandon alone. You know everything I can teach you, but my other grandson hasn't always been here to learn. Do you know what I'm saying?"

Alex nodded slowly, but the hurt, grim look wouldn't leave his face.

"I love you, Grandson," Grandpa said, and hugged him.

Then he went from one member of the family to another and gave each a hug. When he reached my father, he said, "Listen to your son, *Shiye'*. Take time to share the important things you know with him. Some things that are a part of him, he doesn't understand so well yet, but you can make them clear."

Their hug was very long.

"Come on, *Sitsuie*," *Shinali* said, stepping back from my father. "Let's go home."

"Wait," Aunt Ethel said, hurrying into the house. In a minute she came out with a sack. "Some bread and jelly, in case you get hungry, and a thermos of drinking

**132**

water. You'll have to come back over here to wash up in the morning."

I took the sack and we walked away.

Grandpa's house wasn't very far, you could see it from Ethel's place because it was up on a hill. The setting sun made it look even more pink than I remembered it, the windows reflecting an orange-gold glow.

We walked a trail through sagebrush, cedar, and piñon trees with Tailwind, the brown and white dog, following close behind. The sandy path was easy to follow, beaten hard by countless visits back and forth between the homes. As we walked, Grandpa shared experiences he'd had at "that rock" or "under this cedar tree."

When we came out of the cool shadows into the warmth of the sunset and started up the last stretch of hill to the house, *Shinali* stopped talking. He walked even slower, pausing to catch his breath but never for more than a minute, as though determination was compensating for his dwindling strength.

When we got to the woodpile, we stopped at the bent cedar tree. Grandpa stood quietly for a long time, looking at the pink house, the water barrel, assorted crates and tools and junk, the accumulation of a lifetime.

"It's just as I left it," he said. "As though it's been waiting for me."

I helped him to the door, and he gave me the key to the big padlock. I waited at the door while his unsteady hands lit a kerosene lamp. The house had only one room. There were open wooden boxes stacked against the wall to the right, making shelves. A wood stove stood next to the opposite wall, and in the middle of the room there was a table covered with a red and white checked tablecloth. Grandpa's metal bed rested against

**133**

the far wall, under a window. Walking to the table to set down the sack Aunt Ethel had given us, I felt the grit of drifted sand beneath my shoes. My mother once told me that when the wind blows on the reservation, the sand makes a blanket for everything. Seeing the sandy table-cloth helped me understand what she meant. I took the bedspread off the bed and shook it outside. Then Grandpa lay down with a sigh.

"You did it, *Sitsuie*," he said. "You did a hard thing in getting me home. I'm proud of you. No matter what other hard things you have to do in your life, remember this thing that you did, remember the good feeling inside you when the job was done."

*Shinali*'s face, shining with perspiration, looked yellow in the dim light of the small lamp. I got a cup from the box cupboards, blew the sand out of it, and poured him a drink from Aunt Ethel's thermos.

"*Ahe´he, Shiyazhi*," he said and lay back down.

I pulled a wooden chair from the table to the side of the bed so I could be close to him. With his eyes closed, he talked softly in Navajo, and I thought he was talking in his sleep.

In a little while, Grandpa opened his eyes and began to tell me stories about his growing-up years. In story after story he emphasized the importance of relatives, of building on your heritage and your past, of staying true to *important* things. He told me about my father when he was young, how smart and hardworking he was. I saw an image of Keith Rogers that I'd never seen before.

Later, *Shinali* dozed again, and I blew out the lamp. The moon was bright enough that when Grandfather had a coughing spell that lasted several minutes, I could get

**134**

him another drink of water and make sure he was all right.

I leaned back in the chair and closed my eyes, letting myself slip in and out of a light sleep. Every few minutes I'd wake up, hear my grandfather singing or talking softly, and see a new picture of my father in my mind.

# Chapter Fourteen

Suddenly I was awake. I tried to find a reason by searching the early morning murkiness of the room. My ears strained to pick up the rumble of traffic or the whisper of an automatic sprinkling system. Then I remembered I was in Little Water. I sat up straighter in the old chair and rubbed my face. It dawned on me that the room was too quiet. There was no wheeze of labored breathing coming from the bed where Grandpa slept. The jumbled murmur of Navajo words and phrases that had been background noise for my fitful sleep was gone. I held my breath and listened. Nothing. I wanted to get up and check on him, but something kept me sitting there, a feeling of dread that was quickly changing to panic.

"It's time," *Shinali* said into the dim room, and I jumped. His legs sliding off the side of the bed as he sat up covered my relieved sigh. "The sun is probably laughing to himself. You missed the race yesterday and he thinks you're getting lazy."

I stood, rubbing my face again, then walked unsteadily around the room, stretching muscles that sleeping in the uncomfortable chair had wound tight.

Grandpa started to stand and sat back down. "Only one of us is getting lazy," he said, beginning a laugh that disintegrated into a labored coughing spell.

I went over to him and rubbed his frail back until the coughing stopped. It seemed like a futile way to help him, but I didn't know what else to do.

"Just lie back, Grandpa. I'll fix you some breakfast." The bread and jelly that Aunt Ethel had sent with us was still sitting on the table. "After that I'll race that laughing sun while you stay here and rest."

He shook his head. "I want to see you run, *Sitsuie*. When I watch you race, it's like I'm racing myself. I become young again, strong and sure of myself."

He walked slowly toward the door. "Bring the pillow," he said. "And a blanket. There's no use both of us being miserable in the morning cold." Though his back was toward me, I could sense his smile.

As we stepped out the door, Tailwind came up with his head drooping shyly toward the ground, tail wagging. *Shinali* ignored him, holding my arm as we walked across the planks of the porch. "Let's go over there," he said, pointing to a cedar tree.

A moment later he took the pillow from me, laid it against the tree, and slowly sat down. The dog nudged Grandpa's arm and was still ignored. He turned away, followed his tail around in a circle for a few seconds, and settled down.

"It's time to race." *Shinali* looked up at me.

"I'm not sure I know which way to run. I might get lost."

138

"You will know where to go. Run toward the top of that mesa." He pointed at a flat-topped hill about a mile away. "You can see the sky getting light over there. It's the trail your father used to run as a child. As you race, open your eyes, your ears, your heart. Open your lungs to the air and when you greet the sun, let its warmth kindle a small fire within you, a flame that will never go out."

Grandfather took a little leather bag from his shirt pocket, opened it, and dipped his thumb and forefinger inside to get a pinch of its contents. Scattering the yellow powder around, he said some Navajo words. "Corn pollen," he explained. "What I'm doing is not important for you to understand now. Your father will explain it to you if you ask."

He took another pinch of the pollen and sprinkled a few grains on his tongue and forehead, then released what was left into the cool morning air. He looked at me again. "This is important, so listen carefully." He reached over and took my hand. "As you race this morning, Grandson, learn this place well. It's a part of you. Know it so you can take it back with you . . . to your home."

"What are you going to do while I'm racing?"

He smiled. "I'm going to sit here."

"Are you sure you'll be all right? Will you be waiting here when I get back?" The scared feeling was coming back.

"I will always be here."

"I love you, *Shinali*."

"I know, *Sitsuie*. I love you, too."

Reluctantly I turned and started toward the hill, slowly at first, then faster and faster. The smell of my hot,

139

working body pushed out into the cool morning air, mingling with sage and other odors I didn't recognize. Sounds buzzed through my head, a bird, a goat bell, unseen sheep calling from a distant canyon. The bracelet slid up and down my wrist in rhythm with my stride. As I ran, I pictured my grandfather, young and strong, laughing in the joy of running, in the contentment of being who he was. That joy flooded through me and I was Grandpa and I was Brandon and I was my father, grinning and happy and whole, with all the good of his childhood mixing with the hard work and accomplishments of the new life he loved.

As my arms and legs grew heavy, I began to draw in reservation air with short, sharp gasps. I waited for the magic moment, the instant when I would feel light and free, as though I could run forever. When it came, a second feeling came with it. I knew I could keep my promise to *Shinali*. I could make my father see what Grandpa wanted him to understand. If I could just get him to walk along this trail with me, listen to me and to his heart as we walked, Dad would remember the important things.

The sun flashed over the horizon just as I reached the top of the hill. I stopped and leaned on my knees, breathing hard and sweating. Then I looked down from the mesa at sand and red rock, cedar and pine and sagebrush. This was my grandfather's world, my father's world. It was becoming a part of my own world, and I liked its rugged, peaceful beauty.

I started back. Sweat ran in little streams down my face, down my back and chest.

A pain in my side made me stop just before I got back to Grandpa. I walked toward him, waiting for his teas-

**140**

ing voice to encourage me to run. The only sound was the clicking of an insect.

I could see him sitting under the tree, his head resting on his chest. The brown and white dog was nervously pawing at his shoes and whining. At that moment I knew that *Shinali* was no longer really there. An invisible giant hand began to push down on me, making everything inside rush out into the still morning. I didn't plan to cry, but one warm tear clung to the edge of my eyelid, a single tear for all my losses—all the time I hadn't known him, all the things he hadn't had time to teach me, all the empty moments I would feel as time went on.

Sinking to the sand next to him, I took his frail brown hand. We didn't need words anymore. I could feel what he was telling me. "I will always be here. I'm a part of you. Every time you plant a seed or eat oatmeal or ride a bus, I will be there with you. Every time you touch this bracelet you will understand that we are one and it will always be that way."

I knew I'd have to go over to Aunt Ethel's house and tell everyone, but not yet. I held Grandpa's hand for a long time and finally let the tears slide down my cheeks, let them drop from my chin to the land he loved. I thought of what he'd called important things and also the little things: his smile, his songs, his hands moving steadily through soft brown dirt, and those same hands on my shoulders as I worked.

Far off to the east, a hawk circled slowly. "I'm home," Grandpa had said yesterday in the pickup truck as his gaze followed another hawk.

For a long time I watched the bird float freely on warm-air currents, and then I whispered, "You *are* home, *Shinali*. And you have brought me home, too.'' I knew Little Water wasn't really my home, but Grandpa had helped me see that home is not so much a place as it is a feeling. I had to help my dad understand that.

I stood up and started toward Aunt Ethel's house. Tailwind followed me for a little ways, then he stopped and whined. I didn't wait for him, and when I looked around, he was headed back toward Grandpa's.

It was cool and quiet along the trail we had taken the night before. Although people were up and breakfast was started, the little blue house was quiet, too. My mother was standing at the stove next to Aunt Ethel. Dad was sitting at the table. They were the only people in the kitchen/living room, and each of them looked up when I came in the door. I guess they could see in my face that something was wrong. I don't remember what I said, and what followed is a blur of tears and hugging, calling the children from their bedroom, and more tears.

Uncle Stanley and Alex walked in from outside. The tears and hugging started again. In a little while, Stanley said he was going over to Grandpa's house.

''I'll go with you, Stan,'' my dad said.

''Me, too,'' I said.

''No, Brandon.'' My mother was at my side, and with her arm around me, we walked into the other room. ''Stay here and rest a little. From the looks of you, it's been a very long night.''

As I settled onto the bottom bunk, I heard Alex say, ''Can I come, Dad?''

I didn't hear Uncle Stanley's reply, but for the long minutes I lay in that room until sleep finally crept in to keep me company, I didn't see my cousin.

I didn't wake up until noon. By then the Navajo

**142**

police had taken Grandpa to the mortuary in town in their van. My mom and Aunt Ethel took the kids and went to buy new clothes for Grandpa to be buried in. Stanley and Alex took the pickup to get wood. There would be a big meeting of all the friends and relatives to collect money for funeral expenses, and everyone would have to be fed. Dad explained all this to me as we sat outside on the front porch.

"Navajos don't have insurance," he said. "The modern ones do, the ones who work for companies now and don't rely on sheep for their living, but the old-timers, like your grandfather, don't have any." He stared into the distance without seeing the scenery. "Navajos have family instead."

Tailwind sat right in front of me with a pleading look in his eyes, so I scratched him behind the ears and waited for my dad to go on.

"Almost everybody around here is related, if not through blood then through clan or marriage. They'll all be over here tonight to pay their respects to your grandfather and to donate money."

"Sounds kind of nice. Almost better than insurance in a way, more personal."

He looked over at me, then grinned. "We'll talk after the meeting and you can let me know how you feel about it then. Pitching in during troubled times is more personal all right but insurance wins in the efficiency department."

"What do you mean?"

"You'll see," he said.

People started showing up in the late afternoon. They sought out my dad or Ethel and talked with them for a few minutes, then stood around in little groups or returned to sit in their pickups and wait for the meeting to start. The whole area around the house filled up with trucks and people.

"How did all these people find out about Grandpa?" I asked my mother. "These guys don't even have telephones."

"Stanley told a few people and they told a few more and so on."

"What about Uncle Frank and Uncle Arthur?" My father's brothers lived on the reservation but not at Little Water.

"We called them at work. They'll be here in the morning," Mom said.

We watched my father walk from one group to another. He seemed glad to see people, but he couldn't stay still for very long. He finally sat on the porch next to my mother. She rubbed his back, and he smiled over at her.

I was over by the woodpile, playing with the dog, when Aunt Ethel started the meeting. I made Tailwind sit down when she started talking. She spoke in Navajo, but I got the idea that she was thanking everyone for coming. As her speech went on, I recognized the word for father many times. She started crying but went on with the help of my dad's handkerchief.

When she finished, an older man came forward and handed her some money. He gave a speech, too. Then an old woman stood up and talked for a few minutes. The meeting went on that way, one person after another. Some of them handed money to Aunt Ethel, some just stood and talked. Some stood in the crowd to give their speech, others walked up to stand by Ethel.

I wanted to know what they were saying, so I worked

144

my way over toward my father on the porch. Before I got to him, he stood up, whispered something to my mother, and walked around to the back of the house. I threaded my way between visitors to the edge of the crowd. Dad was walking slowly toward *Shinali*'s house. I caught up with him easily.

"Where are you going, Dad?"

"Just walking, getting some fresh air. That's a long time to sit."

"I see what you meant by efficiency."

He grinned at me.

"I still like the feeling of belonging to a family that comes with the inefficiency, though," I said.

"Strange as it may sound, I like that, too." He continued to walk along the trail to Grandpa's house.

"I wish I could understand what everyone is saying."

"They're talking about your grandfather, what a good man he was, how he worked hard, raised a good family." He was silent for a little while. "It's true, you know. He did raise a good family. I wish I could have helped him realize that even his *lost son* was a pretty good person."

When I started to laugh, he glanced over.

"What's funny?"

"That's what he wished about you," I said, and punched his arm. "He wished that he could help you realize that he didn't care whether you lived in Little Water or not, whether you spoke Navajo or wore moccasins or herded sheep. He was proud of you, Dad. He loved you."

"Did he say that?"

I nodded. *"Shinali* said lots of other things, too."

We'd reached the trail where I'd raced the sun that morning. I turned and started up it.

"Where are you going?"

"This is where Grandpa had me race today. I thought I'd look it over one more time."

Dad followed me.

"Grandpa said that no matter how much a person changes, all the experiences he's had and everything he's learned remain a part of him."

"Maybe some of it." My father laughed. "Have you heard me try to speak Navajo?"

He pulled a twig off a sagebrush and held it to his nose. "I used to race the sun along this trail, you know."

"Is the famous yucca plant you sat on along here somewhere?"

He laughed. "I never should have told you that story."

"I'm glad you did. It's a good start. I want to know all your stories."

"All my embarrassing moments?"

"Embarrassing ones, happy ones, sad ones . . . all of them." We passed another sagebrush, and I picked a twig for myself. "All the things that happened from when you were born to right now. They've been a part of what's made you who you are, and since you've been a part of what's made me who I am, I need to know about them."

"*All* the things that have ever happened to me?" Dad laughed. "That's a pretty tall order."

"I don't need to hear them all right now, tonight. We have lots of time."

"I'm not sure I remember very many experiences."

"Grandpa said that you'd remember the important

ones. Just make sure you share them with me when you think of them."

We walked along in silence for a while.

"Is it a deal?" I asked finally.

"Deal," he said, taking my offered handshake, then pulling me into a hug.

After a few more silent yards, I said, "This is as far as I made it this morning."

"Only to here?"

I looked over to catch his grin.

"I'm just kidding," he said. "That's not a bad run . . . of course, I used to make it all the way to the far rim of the mesa most mornings."

"Sure you did, Dad . . . but that was after a unique yucca-spine quickstart!"

As he started to laugh, I turned and jogged back along the trail toward Grandpa's house.

"Hey, wait a minute. Where are you going?"

"No need to wait for old all-the-way-to-the-rim-of-the-mesa Keith Rogers!"

"You're on!" he called, and started running after me.

I've got to admit he was fast and passed me in no time, but he also tired more quickly, so I caught up with him before very long. We stopped running and continued to walk toward the setting sun. We didn't talk, not just because we were winded but because we didn't have to talk. It was a comfortable quiet, like being with *Shinali*.

In a minute, Dad said, "I'd better get back to Ethel's."

"What's your hurry?"

"I'm going to give my old friends a real treat. I'm going to give a speech about all the things your grandfather taught me while I was growing up."

**147**

"They've heard dozens of speeches already."

He grinned. "Not the way I'll say it. I'm going to do it in Navajo . . . and you know my Navajo. They'll be talking for years about Kee Redhouse's arthritic tongue!"

I watched him move along the trail toward Aunt Ethel's house. The sun was just slipping behind the horizon. The sun that I'd raced in the morning and the same sun I'd race tomorrow morning. I stood for a few minutes, taking in the beauty of the changing reds and golds of sunset clouds.

Touching the bracelet Grandpa had given me, I whispered, "This sunset, too, becomes a part of us, *Shinali*. I miss you already, but I know this empty feeling is better than never having you become a part of me." The colors of the sunset swirled together as my eyes filled. Then a tear slid down my cheek, a single warm tear.

# A Glossary
# of Navajo Words

*ahe´he*—thank you

*ayoo deestoi*—It's very hot in here.

*haadee nanina*—Where are you from?

*hagoshii*—OK

*hataathlii*—a singer (in Navajo religion, the medicine man that sings the chants for ceremonies)

*kl´izi yazhi*—little goat

*na´nithkaadi*—sheepherder

*nidaaga*—no

*nizhoni*—beautiful, fine

*shichei*—my grandfather (maternal), also a title of respect for any old person

*shi doo´*—me, too

*shinali*—my grandfather or grandmother (paternal)

*shiyaazh*—my son, when spoken by a woman

*shiyazhi*—my little one

*shiye´*—my son, when spoken by a man

*shizhe´e*—my father

*sik´is*—my friend (person of same gender, man speaking to man, woman speaking to woman)

*sitsuie*—my grandson

*ts´ah*—sagebrush

*ya´at´eeh*—hello (translates: "it is good")